The dog trotted right past Avery and over to me. He was so huge, his head was level with my knees even though I was sitting up on a wall. The dog dropped my sneaker right in my lap, nudged my knee with his nose, and looked up at me with the biggest, softest brown eyes I'd ever seen. A long pink tongue hung out of his mouth and he looked like he was smiling all over his shaggy black face.

My heart nearly leaped out of my chest when he looked at me. It was like we could read each other's minds, and they were saying the same thing: *Hey there, best friend.*

Pet Trouble

Oh No, Newf!

by T. T. SUTHERLAND

SCHOLASTIC INC.
New York Toronto London Auckland
Sydney Mexico City New Delhi Hong Kong

ISBN: 978-0-545-10301-5

12 11 10 9 8 7 6 5 4 3 2 10 11 12 13 14 15/0

Printed in the U.S.A. 40
First printing, February 2010

For Heidi (of course!) ☺

CHAPTER 1

I bet no one at school would believe it if I told them who was with me when I found the dog.

That's because no one knows that we're friends. We're secret friends. We don't talk to each other much at school. It's not my idea. I would totally be friends with him, but he was like, "No, it's lame to be friends with a girl." Which is silly — I have lots of guy friends. But I figured, OK, if that's what he wants.

It's weirder this year, though, because he hardly has any friends at all now. His best friend, Kevin, moved to California over the summer. And I keep telling him he should just sit with us at lunch or talk to me in the hall, but he won't, even though we've been friends since we were super-little. I also tell him he doesn't have to be such a jerk all the time. I bet people would like him better then. But he doesn't care, or he says he doesn't.

Maybe I should back up and tell you more about me.

At the beginning of the school year, our teachers always have us stand up and say something about ourselves. What I should probably always say is: "Hi, I'm Heidi Tyler, and I'm an enormous klutz, so watch out!" I'm serious! I'm the tallest girl in sixth grade. I can't do anything without knocking stuff over or breaking something or spilling ketchup all over myself. I was already the tallest girl by third grade. Isn't that unfair? And I've just kept on getting taller since then. I'm still not used to it. I'm always surprised to find my elbows and head and knees banging into things I don't think they should reach.

And I lose things all the time, too. I'm like the opposite of my mom, who always looks perfect and never loses anything. Can you imagine? Never losing anything? I swear I lose something new every day. I don't know how she does it. Once I tried to follow her around to see if she's keeping notes or something (*Earrings: on the dresser; Shoes: in the hall closet*), but then I kept accidentally bumping into her until finally she was like, "Heidi, would you *please* stop getting underfoot!" (*Daughter: underfoot.*)

Wait, I'm getting distracted. That happens a lot, too, I should warn you. What was I talking about?

Oh, right: my secret friend . . . Avery Lafitte.

I know, it is weird. He's the biggest, meanest bully in the whole class and all my non-secret friends seriously don't like him.

But he wasn't always like that. I know, because I've known him forever.

See, his mom and my mom were best friends in high school. They've always lived right here in our town, and after they met their husbands and got married, they moved into houses right next to each other on the same block just like they always said they would, and then they had babies at the same time, who are Avery and me (well, he's four months older than me, but I'm at *least* four months more mature than him, so there).

Only things didn't go so perfectly from there, at least for his family.

One night when I was four years old, my mom knocked on my door after I'd gone to bed. I wasn't asleep, because I was pretending to read under the covers, which I'd seen a kid do on TV. Only it's harder than it looks because the sheet keeps falling in your face and I was having trouble holding the flashlight and turning the pages all at the same time, plus I'd only just started learning to read so mostly I was looking at the pictures and trying to remember how the kid on TV had juggled everything.

Then came the knock on the door. It startled me so much I jumped, which made me drop the flashlight with a *thunk* on the floor, and then when I leaned over to get it, I fell out of bed with a huge *thud* and then *The Lorax* and all the covers and stuffed animals on the bed came tumbling down on top of me. So when Mom opened the door, I was in a tangled heap on the floor with a flashlight rolling away under the bed.

Mom gave me a confused look.

"Heidi, get back into bed," she said. "Kelly is bringing Avery over."

Kelly is Avery's mom. I'm supposed to call her Kelly instead of Mrs. Lafitte, which is only not weird because I've known her my whole life, so by the time I noticed that it should be weird, I was already used to it.

I rubbed my head where the book had whapped me. "But it's bedtime," I said.

"I know," Mom said, helping me climb back into bed. She shook out the sheets and the blanket and tucked them neatly around me about a zillion times faster than I could have done it. "Avery's staying in here with you tonight."

"Why?" I asked. I sat up in bed and watched her laying out blankets and pillows to make a bed on the floor.

"Because his mom is staying over here, too," Mom said, which totally wasn't an answer.

"Why?" I asked again.

She sighed. "Because Avery's mommy and daddy had a fight. OK?"

I thought about that for a minute while she stuffed pillows into pillowcases. I didn't think I'd ever seen grown-ups fight before.

"Did he pull her hair?" I asked. "Danny Sanchez did that to me last week at preschool and I was *so* mad!"

Mom frowned at me. "Why did Danny pull your hair?"

"Because he's a stupid boy," I said. "And also maybe because I wouldn't let him have the blue Legos."

"Heidi," Mom said, "I thought you were better at sharing than that."

"They weren't for me!" I said. "Charlie was using them to make the ocean! And he's littler than us. So I was helping."

"Hmmm," Mom said. She sat down on the bed beside me. "That does sound helpful. What did you do when Danny pulled your hair?"

Oops. I'd forgotten I wasn't going to tell my mom this story. "Um . . . I kicked him," I admitted. I hid my face behind one of my toy dogs.

"Heidi!" Mom said.

"Sorry," I said. "I guess Kelly didn't kick Avery's dad."

"No," Mom said. She covered her mouth with her hand for a second, then added, "But I think she probably wanted to."

"Why were they fighting?" I asked.

"It doesn't matter," Mom said, kissing my forehead. "I'm sure everything will be better by tomorrow."

A little while later she brought Avery in and showed him where to sleep. He sat down on the blankets and yawned. His hair was all mussed and he was wearing red pajamas with a fire engine on the shirt.

"No talking," Mom warned as she shut the door. "Both of you go to sleep."

I waited until I could see again in the dark. My little night-light shaped like a Saint Bernard was glowing next to my bed, so I could see the lump of gray blankets that was Avery below me. He was lying on his back, looking up at the ceiling. "Hi, Avery," I said.

"Shh," he said. "We'll get in trouble."

"What were your parents fighting about?" I whispered.

There was a long silence. "I dunno," he whispered finally. Another long pause. Then, even more quietly, he added, "Me, probably."

I didn't know if that was true or not, so I didn't know what to say. He turned over so his back was to me and pulled the blankets over his head.

"Hey," I whispered. "You want a dog?"

At first I didn't think he heard me. Then he pushed the covers down a little and rolled over to look at me. "You don't have a dog," he said.

"I have lots of dogs!" I said. I sat up and started piling my stuffed animals around me. "This is Snowball," I said, holding up a fluffy white dog, "and this is Snuffles." I made my wrinkly shar-pei toy walk across my blanket toward him. "And there are lots more — JoJo and Rexie and Mr. Snooper and Hippo —" (I was a little confused when I named that last one. I mean, I *was* four.)

"No," Avery interrupted. "I don't want one." He pulled the blanket over his head again.

This was clearly serious. "OK," I said. "I'll pick one for you." I pulled my favorite dog out of the crowd. He was black and white with floppy ears and a big sweet face and shaggy soft fur and he was very squeezable. I called him Arfer. I thought that was pretty clever, myself.

"Here," I said, leaning over to hand Arfer to Avery. He didn't move. I leaned a bit farther and poked Avery's shoulder with the dog's black nose. "Take him," I said. "This is Arfer."

Avery still didn't move, so I leaned out just a little more to drop it on the other side of him and — bet you can guess — fell out of bed with a yelp, right on top of Avery. Stuffed dogs rained down on our heads.

"OW!" Avery roared, even though I'm sure I didn't hurt him at all.

"Sorry!" I cried, scrambling up again. "Sorry! Sorry!" I could hear my mom's footsteps hurrying to our door. I gathered my dogs up in my arms, leaped into bed, and pulled the covers over my head just before she threw it open.

Avery and I both lay perfectly still, like we were fast asleep already. Which now I realize must have made it extra-obvious that we were pretending, but Mom just went, "Mm-hmm," and shut the door.

"Your fault," Avery whispered.

"Fine, go to sleep," I said. "See if I care." I started arranging my dogs back into their usual sleeping pile. Halfway through, I realized that Arfer was missing.

I peered into the darkness below my bed. A bit of moonlight was coming in the window. Between that and the night-light, I saw that Avery had fallen asleep. He had his arms wrapped around Arfer.

The next day, Kelly and Avery were gone when I woke up. Arfer was gone, too. I hunted through the blankets and under my bed, but all I found was the flashlight with the batteries dead.

I would have asked for him back, but then my mom told me that Avery's parents were still fighting, and that Kelly had taken Avery to his grandma's. And later I saw Avery's mom and dad yelling at each other right in their front yard where everyone could see them. I was so glad that my mom and dad didn't fight like that, I decided maybe it was OK with me if Avery had to keep Arfer until things got better.

And then things never got better. Whenever Mom talks about Avery's family, she just shakes her head and goes, "What a mess." The short version is, his parents got divorced, and then a couple years later they got married again, and then a couple years after that, they got divorced *again*, but they still see each other all the time and mostly they just fight and fight and fight and yell at Avery and send him over to our house to get him out of the way while they fight some more.

It's no fun being Avery. I try to remember that whenever he's super-obnoxious at school. But sometimes I get mad at him and sometimes I say things I feel bad about afterward. Like in the first week of school, when Avery was making fun of Parker Green's new dog. Parker's dog is this gorgeous sunshine-colored golden retriever named Merlin, and he loves Parker so much that he escaped from their yard so he could follow Parker to school on the first day. How cool is that? Parker acted all embarrassed, but I *wish* that was the most embarrassing thing that had ever happened to me!

Anyway, so everyone saw Parker go out to the playground to catch Merlin, and everyone was talking about it. Avery and I even talked about it on the way home from school. He kept saying how funny it was, and then I said I thought Parker was embarrassed, and he got this mean look on his face and right away I said, "Avery, don't. You better not tease Parker about it."

But the very next day, Avery came over to our lunch table and started making fun of Parker, like, "Awww, Parker misses his wittle puppy," stuff like that.

So I got mad — I mean, it was like Avery was *trying* to make me mad, too. And I blurted: "Shut up, Avery. You wish anyone liked you as much as that dog likes Parker."

Well, it worked. It shut him up and he went away. But I felt *so bad* afterward. I felt like the meanest person ever, meaner than Avery ever is. See, you don't even know the saddest part of Avery's story — but I'll get to that later. The point is, I knew it was a really mean thing to say, and I shouldn't have said it. He didn't talk to me for *two weeks*.

Mostly I was busy those two weeks, hanging out with my friend Ella and her dog, Trumpet. I don't know if you can tell from what I've told you so far, but I really *really* love dogs. I want one *so* badly. I've loved them my whole life. If I had a dog, I think I would be happy all the time, just thinking about my dog all day long. I've asked for a dog every year for my birthday and Christmas, but my mom kept saying no. She said they were too messy, and we didn't have time to take care of a dog, and what would we do with it while we're on vacation, and on and on down this whole list of excuses.

So all I could do was hang out with my friends' dogs, and luckily Ella didn't seem to mind me coming over to play with her and Trumpet. Trumpet's a really smart dog. She's a beagle, and she loves to sing along when Ella sings. Ella's a "musical prodigy" — that's what my mom says.

Anyway, so I was at Ella's house a lot, getting ready for the talent show, but whenever I stopped to think about it, I felt bad about being mean to Avery. So when I saw him in his yard the Saturday after the talent show, I figured I should go apologize.

He was bouncing a ball off the old dark green wooden shed at the back of their driveway. He didn't turn around as I came out our back door and went through the gate in the white fence between our yards. I guess maybe he didn't hear me coming, because when I said, "Hi Avery," he jumped, and the ball flew over his shoulder into a bush.

Avery scowled at me. "Look what you did," he said, stomping over to the bush. He picked up a stick and started poking and shaking the branches.

"Hey, you're the one that didn't catch it," I said, trying to be funny. He didn't smile. I got down on my knees and crawled under the bush. Twigs snagged in my hair and I got my elbow stuck in a root, but finally I felt the bumpy rubber under my fingers. I tugged the ball loose and wriggled out into the open again.

"Here you go," I said, tossing it to him. He turned it over in his hands like it had changed into a poodle while he wasn't looking. I stayed sitting on the grass, brushing dirt off my jeans.

"Hey, um," I said. "So, like . . . uh — I just wanted to say I'm sorry."

He squinted at me. His eyes are kind of this neat dark blue color, but I don't think anyone's ever noticed, because he's always scrunching them up to glare at people. "What for?" he grunted.

"You know," I said. "For what I said. A couple weeks ago. In school."

Avery shrugged and threw the ball at the shed again. "Whatever."

"Well," I said. "I mean, I just figured . . . I just wanted you to know, I didn't mean it, and I felt bad because I bet you were thinking about Stitch, too —"

"I don't want to talk about Stitch," Avery said, slamming the ball into the wall and catching it without looking at me.

"OK," I said. I watched him throw the ball a few more times. "Anyway, it's not true. What I said, I mean, about nobody liking you."

"Ha," Avery snorted. "Yeah, except it is."

"Nuh-uh," I said. "People like you."

"No, they don't," he said, "and I don't care anyway."

"Kevin likes you," I said, wrapping my arms around my knees. "And I like you."

"Gross, Tyler," he said. "I don't need to hear about your enormous crush on me. I just ate."

I smiled. That was more like how he normally talked to me. He was always joking about how I was really madly in love with him. (Which, in case you're wondering, is totally not true.)

"Aren't you going to congratulate me on winning the talent show?" I asked.

"That thing is rigged," he said. "Just like *American Idol*."

"Oh, you loved it," I said. "You wanted to take off your shirt and throw it at us like a screaming fan, I bet."

"Well, *that* would have made your day, wouldn't it?" Avery said, and then he kind of smiled, and then we were friends again, and I felt much better.

So that's the important stuff you need to know before I get into the real story. This story begins two weeks later, the day we got detention . . . and met the biggest dog in the world.

CHAPTER 2

Don't get the wrong idea. I'm not, like, a delinquent or anything. I've hardly ever gotten detention, and this time it was really unfair because I was actually trying to *stop* a fight but I got in big trouble anyway, which figures, because if anyone can just fall into a mess, it's me.

It was a Thursday morning, and I was biking to school when I heard my friend Danny Sanchez calling me. I like Danny because he's funny and he's taller than I am. Not many of the kids in my class are taller than me, but Danny and Avery both are, so I don't feel like such a clumsy giant next to them.

Although, of course, the first thing I did when I heard Danny was fall off my bike. Well, it was his fault! He startled me! It was no big deal because I was fine, but I tore a hole in the knee of my new jeans, and I knew my mom wasn't going to be very excited about that. Every time she finds a new hole in my clothes or a new scrape on my shins or a new scuff mark on the wall, she says, "Heidi, you are simply mystifying." I used to think "mystifying" sounded like a good thing, like maybe I could do magic or turn into mist or something, but I've figured out now that what she means is she doesn't understand how anyone can be as much of a ridiculous disaster as I am.

I walked the rest of the way to school with Danny and his friends Parker, Troy, and Eric. Danny just got a new dog, too, and I hadn't even met her yet, and then they told me that *Eric* got a new dog as well, and it was like *torture* that all my friends could have dogs and I couldn't. But Danny said I could come to the park with them after school if I wanted and I was like, *YES PLEASE DOGS NOW PLEASE YES.*

But that was before we got to school and things started to go terribly wrong.

We could hear shouting from the sixth-grade hallway as we went through the front doors, and I could tell that one of the people shouting was Rory Mason. Rory is one of my best friends. She sang "Leader of the Pack" in the talent show with me and Ella. We have this plan where after high school the two of us are going to backpack around New Zealand together jumping out of planes and spelunking in dark caves and stuff, because I know she wouldn't be scared to do any of that and I figure that'd make me braver, too.

Then I realized that the other person shouting was Avery, and I was like, *Oh, no.* Every time Avery gets in trouble at school, his parents get super-mad and then there's even *more* yelling and fighting, and then he's grumpy for months afterward. So you'd think he would try harder not to get in trouble, but sometimes it's like trouble just falls on him. I don't mean accident-trouble, like what happens to me. I mean, if someone's going to pick a fight or if someone's going to get blamed for something, it's probably Avery.

Also, I know Rory, and she pretty much says what she really thinks, and she would totally not be afraid of hitting him. Plus, I didn't need my best friend and my secret friend hating each other's guts. It's hard enough to stop Avery from complaining about everyone at school.

"She says you took it, Avery!" Rory yelled as we came up to the crowd that was standing around our lockers. I saw Rory's little stepsister, Cameron, standing behind her, looking all mad, so I figured that was the "she" Rory was talking about. That meant real trouble because Rory is like a Rottweiler about defending Cameron (who is eight) and her brother, Cormac (who is six).

"I didn't!" Avery yelled back. "She's lying!"

"Cameron wouldn't lie!" Rory shoved him in the chest.

"Yeah!" Cameron yelled. "So there! Meanie!"

"I don't need her stupid lunch money!" Avery shouted. He looked really upset. His green polo shirt was coming untucked and he kept clenching and unclenching his fists. I know that makes him look like he's about to punch someone, but I think it actually means he's trying to stop himself from getting too mad.

"Give it back, Avery!" Danny called.

I thought that was kind of unfair. We didn't even know the whole story yet. Danny is like that sometimes. He jumps right into action without thinking about what he's doing or what other people might feel. I mean, he's my friend, but sometimes I think he needs to be careful he doesn't become a more popular version of Avery.

Besides, here's something to know about Avery. Yeah, I know, he's a bully and he says mean things and he likes making other people as miserable as he is. But he's not a liar, and he's not a thief. I was pretty sure about that.

"Yeah, Avery, stop being a jerk!" Tara Washington shouted. Like she should talk, by the way. She is *absolutely* as mean as Avery when she wants to be.

Then Brett Arbus poked his nose in and offered to buy Cameron's lunch in his smiley, slippery way. I don't really get Brett. I know the other girls think he's cute, but I think he has shifty eyes. Plus, I've seen him wrinkle his nose at me a couple of times when I've fallen over in the cafeteria and spilled my lunch tray everywhere. So I know he has a low tolerance for klutzes, which means we definitely wouldn't get along.

"It's not about the money," Rory said. "It's about pushing around a little girl! What kind of freak-show coward are you, Avery?"

Well, OK. So then I had to get involved. Didn't I? I mean, poor Avery, if he was innocent. Or if he wasn't, then Rory needed my help.

I jumped in and grabbed Avery's arm. "Stop fighting!" I said. "You guys are both going to get in trouble again!" Avery shook me off and kicked Yumi Matsumoto's locker really hard with his boot. I was surprised he didn't leave a dent. If I'd tried to do that, by the way, I would have fallen over *and* sprained my ankle, most likely.

"I didn't steal any stupid lunch money," Avery growled, glaring at Rory.

"Cameron says he did!" Rory insisted. "Why would she lie about that?"

OK, I had to admit that was pretty confusing. "Maybe there's a mistake," I said. "Hey, Cameron, did you maybe just lose it?"

"No!" Cameron said, pouting. Cameron is a very cute third-grader. She looks like a miniature Nicole Kidman, with perfect pale skin and vibrant red curls. But I'm afraid being that cute helps her get away with anything. I mean, I would never tell Rory that her sister is a bit spoiled, but . . . she kind of is. "It was in my backpack and then it was gone! He took it!" Cameron said decisively.

"Out of your backpack?" Rory said. "I thought you said he took it from you."

Oh, I thought. *So it could be a mistake.* I tried to give Avery a reassuring look, but he was too busy scowling at Cameron to meet my eyes.

"He did!" Cameron said. "It was mine!"

"But did you see him take it out of your backpack?" I asked.

Cameron's blue eyes were filling with tears, but I've seen her do that lots of times to get what she wants, so I wasn't sure it was all that real. "I know he did!" she cried. "I know he took it! He's mean!"

I couldn't really argue with that, but I could see that Rory was confused, too. She'll do anything for Cameron and Cormac, but she's also really fair. I knew she wouldn't have accused Avery if she hadn't been sure he did it. And now she wasn't so sure.

That's when we heard the dreaded sound of Vice Principal Taney's voice.

"What is all this?" he barked, hurrying toward us. He looked *really* mad, almost as mad as he was when someone hit him with a piece of bologna during the cafeteria food fight a couple weeks earlier. I felt like my feet were frozen in place. It was like someone just piled a whole pack of Great Danes on my shoulders. I was too terrified to move.

Rory and Avery and Cameron were stuck there, too, but everyone else vanished like they'd been Hoovered up by an invisible vacuum cleaner. I didn't blame them — I'd have run away from Mr. Taney, too, if I could — but still, thanks a lot, *Danny*, for sticking around to defend me.

Mr. Taney has long, bony fingers. He was wagging one of them at us like he was hoping it would turn us all into salamanders.

"Sir, it's just a misunderstanding—" I said as fast as I could. "Really, there's nothing wrong, everyone's—"

"Detention!" Mr. Taney shouted. "All of you!" He stopped in front of us. His white hair was sticking up in grouchy tufts. There was a spot of toothpaste on his mustard-yellow striped tie.

"All of us?" Cameron squeaked, looking outraged. "That's not fair! *I* didn't do anything! I'm a good girl!"

Mr. Taney dislikes all the students, but unlike most people in the world, I think he hates the littler ones even more than the big ones. He pointed his bony forefinger at her little button nose. "Detention," he snarled. He pointed it at Rory, then Avery, then me. "Detention. Detention. Detention."

"Can't we explain—" Rory started to say, but Mr. Taney cut her off.

"My office. Lunch," he snapped. "And you all have after-school detention for the next week."

"A whole *week*!" Cameron shrieked.

"Push me, and I'll make it two," Mr. Taney hissed. "Now get to class."

So that's how I ended up in detention with Rory and Avery after school that Thursday. See? It wasn't really my fault, right? But maybe it's good that I was there, because Rory and Avery kept throwing each other these fierce hostile looks, and I'm not sure they could have stayed quiet that whole time if I wasn't sitting in between them trying to block the angry vibes.

And in some ways, it's definitely good that I got detention, because of what happened on the way home.

Avery rocketed out of his seat the minute Mr. Guare told us we could go. I don't even think he stopped at his locker. He shot out the front door of the school, practically leaving puffs of smoke behind him like a cartoon.

Rory and Cameron walked me to my locker and then stood well back so nothing would fall out of it onto their heads. I don't have any idea how my locker becomes so messy so quickly, but I never have time to clean it and, anyway, at least I know everything's in there somewhere. I hope.

"You want a ride home?" Rory asked me as I untangled my sweater from my math book and spilled jelly beans all over the hall. "I can't promise it'll be fun. Dad's not happy at all."

"It's not my *fault*," Cameron said for the eightieth time. "Avery's mean. I *know* he took my lunch money."

Rory didn't bother answering her.

"That's OK," I said. "I brought my bike today."

"All right," Rory said, pulling her ponytail tighter. "See you tomorrow, Heidi. Sorry about detention."

"It's no big deal," I said. "I finished most of my homework, so it's not all bad." I smiled at Rory to show her I knew it wasn't her fault.

Rory took Cameron's hand and they went off down the hall toward Coach Mason's office. I wrestled with my locker until I got it shut, and then I went out the front door and unlocked my bike. It was the last one there. I hung my shiny blue helmet on the handlebars and pushed it across the street.

There's a big field across from the school with a track running around it, which grown-ups use a lot for exercise. You can usually find someone jogging there, wearing sweatpants and headphones and a determined look, but this afternoon it was empty. Trees and thick bushes grow around the edges, hiding the field from the streets around it, and there's a big space in the middle that the town uses for summer sports. I play soccer there a lot.

My bike went *bump bump bump* over the dirt as I pushed it toward the low wall that runs along one side of the track, under the trees. Avery was sitting on the wall, throwing stones at a tree trunk.

Sometimes he waits for me there so we can walk home together.

"I have this great idea," he said as I walked up. "Let's take that lunch money I 'stole' and run away to New York City and never come back."

"I know you didn't steal it," I said. I dropped my bike on the grass and hopped up on the wall next to him. "Are your parents going to be really mad?"

"Well, Dad's staying in a hotel again this week," Avery said, "so maybe she won't tell him, since they're 'not speaking.' But Mom —" He threw another stone, really hard, and it bounced off the bark with a *clunk*.

"Maybe if you explain it to her . . . That it was a mistake . . . " I said. "I can talk to her if you want."

"Whatever," Avery said. "It's not worth it. If she wants to get mad, fine. I don't care. That stupid little *brat*." He jumped down, picked up a handful of rocks, and tossed them all at once. *Blip blip bonk bonk bonk* they went as they pinged off the tree and scattered to the ground.

I didn't argue with him. If I tried to defend everyone Avery gets mad at, or if I tried to defend him to all my other friends, I'd never have time for anything else. "Why do you think Cameron said it was you?" I asked.

Instead of answering, he shoved his hand in his pocket, pulled out a small white object, and tossed it at me. I lunged to catch it and would have fallen off the wall, but Avery caught my arms and pushed me back up.

"There you go, throwing yourself at me again," he said, rolling his eyes.

"Thanks," I said with a grin, peering at the thing in my hand. It was an eraser, little and white and shaped like a tiny white dog — some kind of terrier, I guessed, with a red collar around its neck and a little pink tongue hanging out. "This is so cute," I said.

"I thought you'd like it," Avery said with a shrug. I looked up in surprise, and he went, "Don't get all mushy-wushy on me, Tyler. I found it on the playground yesterday. Problem is, the brat saw it at the same time and she pitched a fit when I wouldn't let her have it." He poked a finger in one ear and turned it, scrunching up his face. "Man, she's loud. I told her to go annoy someone else and left her there screaming. Anyway, I guess that's why she's mad at me."

"Do you think she made it all up?" I asked.

He shrugged. "Either way, she's an annoying brat."

"Wow," I said, flipping the eraser between my

fingers. "So you won this in a fight with an eight-year-old girl. No *wonder* I have such a crush on you."

"Shut up," he said, grabbing my foot and pulling off my sneaker.

"Give that back!" I yelled as he ran off across the field. "I'm not going to chase you with one shoe, Avery! Get back here!"

"What, this?" he called, stopping several feet away. He tossed my shoe from one hand to the other. "You want this?"

I crossed my arms. "I'm not going to come after it," I said.

"OK," he said with a shrug. "Then we can just stay here forever. Suits me. *I* don't want to go home."

Rrrrrrooorrrroorrrrroooooo.

I tilted my head at Avery. "Did you just growl at me?" I asked. I was sure I'd heard something — something like a growl or a whimper or a mumble. Had it come from the bushes by the wall? Some of them had thick leaves and overgrown vines tangled around them. Was there an animal hiding in one of them?

"You're losing it, Tyler," Avery said, wiggling his finger by the side of his head like I was crazy.

"You didn't hear that?"

"I didn't hear anything," he said with another shrug. He tossed my shoe behind his back and caught it in his other hand, then waved it at me.

"We shouldn't be late for dinner," I said, deciding to ignore the weird noise in the bushes. "Then we'll get in even more trouble."

"Bet my mom wouldn't notice," he said.

"Bet she *would*," I said. "Avery, give me back my sneaker."

"Nope," he said, dancing back another step.

"You're a pain in my butt," I said.

"That's why you're in looooooooove with me," he said. "Hey, do you know you're wearing two different-colored socks?"

I looked down and realized that my shoeless foot was wearing a dark blue sock, while the other one was wearing a yellow sock with black polka dots. How had I done that? I must have been in such a hurry that morning that I hadn't even noticed. My room is always kind of a mess, no matter how much my mom yells at me to clean it. It's easy to get things mixed up in there.

"Yeah, I did that on purpose," I said.

"Sure you did," he said.

"If you don't give me back my shoe right now," I

said, "I'm going to tell everyone at school that *you're* secretly in love with *me*."

"Like anyone would believe that, when I'm so far out of your league," Avery said, but he was frowning. "Hey, I have an idea. Since you like dogs so much, how about, if you want it — then you can fetch it!" He turned and threw my sneaker as hard as he could. It flew up in a huge arc, up and up and up and way out across the field.

"Avery!" I shouted, but then suddenly there was a huge rustling sound, and something exploded out of the bushes. A blur of black-and-white fur flew out, shot past Avery, and zoomed across the grass. Before my sneaker even hit the ground, the fur blur was half-way to where it was going to land.

I gasped.

It was a dog — the biggest, furriest dog I'd ever seen.

Avery's mouth was wide open. I'm sure mine was, too. We stared as the dog pounced on my sneaker, wrapped his massive jaws around it, and came trotting back toward us. His glorious black tail swung back and forth like a giant flag in a parade. He held his head up high and his long fur swished shaggily as he pranced over the grass.

He was *gorgeous.*

The dog trotted right past Avery and over to me. He was so huge, his head was level with my knees even though I was sitting up on a wall. The dog dropped my sneaker right in my lap, nudged my knee with his nose, and looked up at me with the biggest, softest brown eyes I'd ever seen. A long pink tongue hung out of his mouth and he looked like he was smiling all over his shaggy black face.

My heart nearly leaped out of my chest when he looked at me. It was like we could read each other's mind, and they were saying the same thing: *Hey there, best friend.*

CHAPTER 3

"Well, hi there," I said, holding my hand out to the dog. His tail wagged harder as he sniffed my fingers thoroughly and then licked them.

Avery came a bit closer, staying out of the dog's reach. "What — where did that — what *is* that?" he asked.

"It's a dog," I said, and Avery snorted. The dog started rubbing his massive head against my knees and I buried my hands in his fur to scratch behind his ears. "It's the best dog in the world. Thank you for bringing me my sneaker, best dog ever."

"That's not a dog," Avery said. "That's, like, a bear cub or something."

"It's a Newfoundland," I said. "They're amazing dogs. The dog in *Peter Pan* was a Newfoundland — you know, the one that took care of the kids before they went off to Neverland."

"Uh, wrong, Tyler," Avery said. "I saw that movie. It was a Saint Bernard."

I rolled my eyes at him. "Yeah, in the *movie*. In the *book*, which came *first*, Nana was a Newfoundland."

"Whatever," said Avery. "You read too much." He stared at me as I pulled my sneaker on. It was a little slobbery, but I didn't care. I hopped off the wall and knelt beside the dog, who leaned toward my face for a minute, sniffing, and then slurped his tongue up my cheek. I laughed and rubbed his solid white neck and chest. I read somewhere that dogs like that. He sure seemed to; his tail went *flap flap flap* and I could practically feel the breeze it made.

"Hey there, handsome," I said to him. "Are you the best dog ever? Did you teach Avery a lesson about stealing my shoe? Yes, you did! What are you doing out here? Aren't you the handsomest? How did you get to be so handsome?" And other stuff along those lines. That's pretty much what happens to me whenever I'm around dogs. I get all googly and say whatever pops into my head (well, OK, maybe that's not so different from how I usually am). And right then I was too happy to think straight. I just wanted to throw my arms around the dog and never let go of him. He had the sweetest face I'd ever seen and I felt like he loved me already and I was, like, ready to jump out of an airplane for him or whatever I needed to do to keep him.

But a dog this beautiful had to belong to somebody. Surely a jogger would come running along any moment to take him back, waving the leash he'd escaped from.

"I think that thing is bigger than a Saint Bernard," Avery said.

"Are you bigger than a Saint Bernard?" I said to the dog. "And smarter? And handsomer? Are you the most amazing dog that ever lived?"

"Oh, brother," Avery said. "And I thought you were soppy about *me*."

The dog's coat was black and white, kind of like a panda's, with pretty black splotches on his white legs. As I looked him over, I noticed his paws were caked with mud and his fur was matted and tangled. I ran my hand down his side and realized he was really thin. I could feel his ribs even through his thick fur. It made me hurt inside, like when I eat too much candy (which happens way too often), but in my heart instead of in my stomach. How could anyone have a dog this beautiful and not take care of him? He licked my face again and pressed himself closer to me. He just wanted to be loved. I knew that feeling.

“This poor dog,” I said to Avery. “Look how thin he is. Don’t your owners feed you, sweetheart?”

Reluctantly, I felt around his neck, looking for a collar. If there was an address on it, I’d have to take him back to his owners . . . even though they clearly didn’t deserve him. At first I thought the collar was just buried in his shaggy fur. Then I realized he wasn’t wearing one at all. My heart jumped up and thumped against my chest. Maybe . . . maybe I could *keep* him!

Then my heart tumbled down to earth again. There was no way my mom would let a dog this huge and shaggy into her perfect house. This dog was pretty much the exact opposite of everything my mom wanted our house to be.

“There’s no collar,” I said to Avery. He came closer and reached out his hand. The dog sniffed him, licked his fingers, and then turned back to me.

“Guess he likes you best,” Avery said. “Figures.”

I put my hands on either side of the dog’s face and rumpled his fur. “I like you, too, you big furry thing.” He licked my nose and I laughed.

“Gross,” Avery said, but I knew he didn’t mean it. He wouldn’t really mind at all if the dog licked his face.

“What should we call him?” I said, rubbing the dog’s sides.

“Call him?” Avery said. “Why would we call him anything?”

The dog snuffled in my hands, and I remembered that I had dog treats in my bag. I know, it’s crazy to have dog treats and no dog, but I buy them with my own allowance and carry them around so that I can say hi to all the dogs I meet and then they’ll like me. For instance, they came in handy when I first met Trumpet. I pulled my bag closer and started digging through it. The Newfie tried to poke his nose inside, nudging my hands.

“Oh, hello, bossy,” I said to him. “No, no you don’t.” I snatched the candy bar out of his teeth before he could tear it open. “This isn’t for you,” I said to him. “Chocolate bad! Bad for dogs. *This* is for you.” I zipped open the bag of treats and he got *super*excited. His whole body wriggled and then he tried to climb all the way onto my lap, which was a hilariously bad idea, considering he was literally bigger than me.

“Ack!” I yelped. “Wait! Back! Goofy dog! Quit it!” His enormous white paws landed on my shoulders and knocked me over onto my back. He bounced over me and tried to jump at the bag of treats, which

I was holding out of his reach. I rolled away from him and got to my knees, but he bundled right into me and knocked me over again. He was such a ball of love and fur and joy and excitement that I didn't even care when he accidentally stepped on my hair or that I was getting my clothes all dirty. It was like play-wrestling with the Abominable Snowman.

I felt the bag of treats get whisked out of my hand and then the dog's weight disappeared from on top of me. I sat up, expecting to see the dog wolfing down the treats and probably the bag as well, but instead I saw Avery standing up on the wall, holding the treats out of the dog's reach. The dog went "WOOOOOF," in this really deep, velvety voice. He tried to jump up and grab the bag. Avery held it a bit higher and peered at me.

"I just saved you from a dog trampling," he said. "Yeah, I know, I'm your hero, try not to faint."

"Oh, you know you're my hero, Avery," I said. I climbed up on the wall beside him and took a treat out of the bag. "All right, Yeti," I said to the dog. "Sit." I held the treat out over the dog's nose.

"What did you call it?" Avery asked. The dog paced back and forth below us, his eyes fixed on the treat in my hand.

"Yeti," I said. "Doesn't he look like a yeti?"

"No," said Avery. "Since you made that word up."

"I did not!" I said. "Yeti, sit." I moved the treat over the dog's head. This had totally worked with Ella's dog, Trumpet. That beagle sat almost right away. But the Newfoundland just backed up so he could keep looking at the treat. "A yeti is like Bigfoot, or the Abominable Snowman," I said to Avery. "It's a big furry creature that lives in the mountains. I think. Anyway, I thought it sounded like a good name. Come here, Yeti."

The dog obediently took a few steps toward me. This time when I moved the treat ovcr his head, Yeti followed it with his eyes instead of stepping back. His head tipped back to watch it, and then his butt slowly sank to the ground, and he sat.

"Good boy!" I said. "Good boy, Yeti!" I gave him the treat, which he scarfed down the way I eat M&M's — as fast as possible. He swiped his tongue over his nose and jowls and tilted his head at me hopefully. His long, shaggy black ears hung down on either side of his head, with little muddy tendrils at the bottom. His eyes went from my face to the bag of treats and back again like, *Hello? More treats? I think I'm being pretty clear here!*

"OK, crazy person," Avery said. "You can't name this dog. He's not yours."

"Well, he's not anybody's right now," I said. "Maybe he could be mine."

Avery gave me a look, and I knew he was thinking what I was — my mom would have a heart attack if I brought this dog home.

"Maybe you could take him, then," I suggested.

"Oh, no," he said. "My house is no place for dogs."

I knew what he meant. And his mom would be no more psyched about a dog than my mom, especially on a day when Avery got detention.

"We can't just leave him out here," I said. "Poor hungry dog." I made Yeti sit again and gave him another treat. He licked my hand so sadly afterward that I held out the bag and just let him eat them all. He plunged his nose into the bag and his tail started whizzing back and forth. *Worf worf snorf*, he went, lapping them up.

"Well," Avery said, "you're going to have a hard time getting rid of him now, idiot."

"Isn't there somewhere we could hide him, just for a little while?" I said. "Then we could at least feed him properly while we look for his owners. And maybe if I work on my mom — if I convince her . . ."

"Yeah, right," said Avery. "There's no way your mom would say yes to this guy. And good luck hiding him. What are you going to do, stuff him in your backpack? Maybe you haven't noticed this, but he's *gigantic.*"

I jumped off the wall again and stood next to Yeti, patting his head and sides. He leaned against me and made a contented noise, like *huffle.* Where could we hide a dog this big? Nowhere in my house, that's for sure. We'd never get him from the door to my room without being spotted by my mom, who watches every move I make like a hawk, just in case I'm about to break something. And with Avery in such trouble, we couldn't risk trying to sneak the dog into his house either.

"Oh!" I said suddenly, making the dog start. "I know! I've got it! Avery, we'll hide him in your shed! You know, the one behind your driveway — the one your parents never use. Nobody ever looks in there. We can bring him food and water and take care of him until we figure out what to do next."

Avery was shaking his head. "You're nuts. Round the bend, Tyler. They'll catch us for sure."

"Bet you they won't," I said. "And if they do, I'll take the blame, I promise. Come on, Avery. He needs our help. Look at these eyes." Yeti helpfully gave Avery a big-eyed, woeful expression. "If Stitch were out on the street and someone found him," I said, "wouldn't you want them to —"

"All *right*, all right," Avery interrupted quickly. "Just shut up about it. We can stick him in the shed, but just for a couple of days. Come on, let's go." He grabbed his backpack, shoved his hands in his jacket pockets, and stomped off. I realized it was starting to get dark. The sky was pink and purple above the trees and it was getting colder.

"Don't worry, Yeti," I said, stroking the smooth black fur on his head. "You'll stay somewhere warm tonight, and we'll feed you, and it'll all be OK."

Yeti looked up at me trustingly, and as I started to push my bike out of the field, he stayed close to my other side, padding happily through the grass.

I had no idea what I was going to do next. I was going to be in big trouble if Mom found out about this. But Yeti needed me, so whatever trouble was coming my way, I could handle it.

That's what I hoped anyway.

CHAPTER 4

We crept up to our houses quietly. The streetlights on our block cast warm yellow circles on the sidewalk. Through the window, I could see my mom in our kitchen, watering her plants and cleaning the counters. Avery's mom was sitting in their living room. I could tell she was watching TV because of the blue light glowing on her face.

I lowered my bike onto my front lawn, and then Avery and I ran up his driveway with Yeti galloping along beside us. The Lafittes don't have a garage. Their driveway runs between his house and mine, with the white fence and a patch of grass with yellow flowers separating it from our driveway.

Behind the house, his driveway turns and ends at this old shed. The shed used to be green with bright white shutters around the one window and white shingles on the slanting roof, but now it's all kind of faded and dingy.

They used to keep things in there like the lawn mower and Mr. Lafitte's tools and his woodworking set, but during one of their big fights Kelly sold them all on eBay because "he never even used them, the lazy jerk." Mr. Lafitte was pretty mad about that, so then he turned around and sold her car, and then there was a day when all of Mr. Lafitte's clothes ended up on the front lawn, and that was about when they got divorced for the second time.

Anyway, now Kelly pays people to mow the lawn or fix things around the house. So there's nothing in the shed but old sawdust and cobwebs on the rickety shelves. I sneezed as Avery pulled open the door.

"Shhh," he said fiercely.

"Sorry," I said. I led Yeti inside and he put his nose down, sniffing along the floor. I laughed when he sneezed, too. "Here you go, Yeti. Good boy. We'll be back soon with water and food."

"Uh, *you* might be," Avery said. "I'll be sent to my room for the rest of the night."

"It's OK, I'll take care of him," I said. "Thanks, Avery."

"Bleargh," he said. "You're such a sap, Tyler."

Poor Yeti tried to follow us out the door. I said, "No, sweetheart, stay," and pulled the door closed. There was a latch to hold it in place, but it still hung open a crack. Of course, Yeti couldn't fit through such a narrow space, but he stuck his huge black nose to the opening and went *Urroorroooorrrroooo.*

"Oh," I said, clutching my chest. "I'm so sad! I want to let him come inside and sleep on my bed! Poor sad dog."

"Not me," Avery said. "He's a muddy mess. And so are you, by the way."

I looked down and realized he was right. I was covered in smudges of dirt and long black dog hairs. Not to mention the hole in my jeans that I'd torn when I fell off my bike that morning.

"Oh, man," I said, brushing frantically at my shirt. "Mom is going to faint when she sees me like this."

Avery reached over and pulled some twigs out of my hair. "Well, it's your problem," he said gruffly. "See you around."

"Yeah, sure. Thanks again," I said, hurrying back down his driveway. When I looked back, I saw him scratching his head, and then he sighed and trudged up his back steps. I felt bad for him. I knew he was going to have a rough night getting yelled at by his mom.

I grabbed my bike and pushed it into our garage through the side door. I didn't turn on the light, in case Mom looked out the window and noticed it.

There was light coming in from the streetlights outside and from Avery's house, so I could see a little. But I had to be really quiet, because the door from the garage goes right into the kitchen, and I didn't want my mom to hear me.

As silently as I could, I scrounged through some of the boxes until I found two large ceramic bowls packed in a cardboard box in lots of brown scrunchy paper. They were totally hideous — gray and knobbly and misshapen with big red dots on the outside and a pale greenish color on the inside.

The box wasn't labeled. My guess was that they were presents or something that Mom didn't want, so she'd put them in the garage until she figured out what to do with them. There's a lot of random stuff in our garage. It's mostly all neatly organized and labeled, but my parents hardly ever go in there unless they need something specific. They probably wouldn't even notice the bowls were gone.

Next, I searched through the plastic bins on the back shelves until I found one labeled BLANKETS. "Perfect," I whispered, dragging out the top blanket. It was red and black and yellow in a pattern of fuzzy squares. Underneath it was one of the blankets I used to drag around when I was little. It was pink with a little black poodle in each corner.

In case you're wondering, all my dog toys and things didn't come from my parents. They didn't want to "encourage my obsession." But my grandpa — Mom's dad — loves giving me dog presents. He grew up with dogs, but he couldn't have any as a grown-up, mainly because Grandma was allergic to them and also didn't like them very much. After she died, he talked about getting one, but he travels a lot for his job, so he still hasn't.

And once everyone saw him giving me stuffed dogs and paw-print outfits and books like *Clifford the Big Red Dog*, and *Harry the Dirty Dog*, and *Love That Dog* by Sharon Creech, the rest of our relatives started doing the same thing, thinking it was some kind of theme. This made me totally happy, but every time I got a new one, my mom would shake her head and say, "Quit giving her ideas, Aunt May," or "Thanks a lot, Dad," or whatever.

This blanket was from another aunt, Dad's sister, Jennifer, and I'd dragged it around the house with me for at least a year before Mom made it "disappear" into the garage. I pulled out a third blanket and wrapped them all around one of the bowls. Then I filled the other bowl with water from the tap on the outside wall of our garage, the one Mom usually attaches the hose to when she waters the garden.

It sounded so loud in the quiet dusk. I was sure someone would poke her head out any minute and ask what I was doing. It also splashed all over the place, so by the time the bowl was full, I was pretty wet.

I picked up the blanket-wrapped bowl under one arm and carried the water bowl carefully over to the fence. I set it down as I went through the gate and somehow managed not to step in it or knock it over or anything. I was moving pretty slowly, although my heart was racing. I just wanted to get the water and blankets to Yeti before anyone caught me.

He still had his nose pressed to the crack in the door, and he must have smelled me coming because I heard his tail start thumping against the door. He made a little excited noise when I unlatched the door and edged inside. Yeti kind of bounced his front paws up and down, like he was ready to play. I set the water bowl down and he buried his face in it, slurping and spraying water as he drank. While he did that, I spread out the blankets and tried to arrange them in a comfortable nest for him.

Yeti came over as I finished and put one shaggy paw on the blankets, sniffing them.

"Yeah, that's for you," I said, scratching behind his ears. He noticed the other bowl and nosed it, licked the bottom of it, and then looked at me like, *I think you forgot something.*

"I know," I said. "I'll bring you food just as soon as I can sneak out, OK? Stay here and wait for me."

Yeti flopped down on the blankets with a sigh. I patted his head, and he inched toward me, pulling himself forward with his front paws.

"Poor good boy," I said. "I'll be back as soon as I can."

Hrrrrrfle snuffle, went Yeti. His fur was so warm and soft. I just wanted to curl up and rest my head on his side and fall asleep right there with him.

But I had to get home for dinner. I latched the door behind me again and ran back to the gate. As I went through, I heard shouting coming from Avery's kitchen window.

"What is wrong with you?" his mom yelled. "Why can't you even *try* to stay out of trouble?"

I didn't want to hear any more. I closed the gate and went through the garage, opening the kitchen door with my key.

"Oh, there you are, Heidi," my mom said without turning around. She was bending over to peer inside the oven. Our kitchen is very white — white cabinets, white counters, white ceiling — with shiny steel appliances and a pretty gray-and-blue Greek design for the backsplash tiles. Plants fill the big window over the sink, like basil and rosemary and a small lemon tree, all stuff my mom uses for cooking. The room was warm and cozy and it smelled like roast chicken and golden potatoes. I stopped in the doorway to breathe in deeply. That was my mistake. I should have run upstairs right away.

"Your principal called to tell me you had detention, but I didn't understand what she was saying at all," my mom said. "Something about a fight in the hallway? That didn't sound like — HEIDI ABIGAIL TYLER!"

I jumped. Mom had straightened up and was staring at me with her hand pressed to her open mouth.

"Heidi! What did you *do* to yourself?"

I stood on tiptoe to peek into the mirror in the hallway. My hair was a wild snarly mess, which is pretty normal because I can't ever find my brush in the morning. It doesn't usually have quite so many bits of tree stuck in it, though. My face was smeared with dirt, and my peach-colored long-sleeved shirt had a little rip in the shoulder and my jeans were dripping wet mud all over Mom's clean floor.

"Oops," I said, trying to comb out the tangles in my hair with my fingers. "Sorry, Mom." I hopped onto the welcome mat at the back door and tried to wipe off my muddy sneakers.

Mom seemed at a loss for words. She kept starting sentences and then not being able to finish them. It was like she'd been expecting a silky cocker spaniel to walk through the door but she got a wildebeest instead.

Mom looks like an actress from an old movie. She has dark brown hair that's straight until it flips up perfectly at the ends, and she wears a lot of pretty patterned skirts and dresses with plaids or polka dots or flowers, which I could never do because I'd match them with the wrong color shoes or a too-wide belt or something, but on her they always look perfect. She's definitely the prettiest mom I know, and she's probably the smartest, too. She has a PhD in art history and everything, plus she's always using words like "mystifying" and "flabbergasted" and "irreparable damage."

Finally she said, "I don't know whether to ask you what happened or send you right upstairs to get cleaned up. Does your appearance have anything to do with your detention? Did you really get in a fight?"

"No!" I said quickly. "I was trying to stop a fight; that's why I got detention. This — um — I fell off my bike." Well, that was true. That explained part of it anyway. I carefully left out how that had been in the morning, so she'd think it had just happened.

"Into a swamp?" my mom asked drily, whisking open a drawer and pulling out an old towel. "Here, take off your shoes and towel off your feet so at least you won't track mud all through the house. And while you're doing that, tell me about the fight."

I stuffed my mismatched socks — Mom raised her eyebrows at those — into my damp sneakers and rubbed my feet and jeans with the towel while I told Mom all about Avery and Rory and the lunch money and how it wasn't really Avery's fault and how Cameron was probably just confused and about Mr. Taney being all mad so even Principal Hansberry couldn't get us out of detention although it sure seemed like she understood what had happened.

Mom was nodding as I finished the story. "I got the impression she felt you were being unfairly punished," she said. "Do you want me to talk to Mr. Taney?"

"No, that's OK," I said. "It'll only make him madder and he'll get me for something else. Anyway, I should stick with Avery and Rory."

Mom patted my head with a smile. "You're a good kid, Heidi." Then her gaze went to my jeans and she frowned. "Is that —" She reached down and poked the tiny glimpse of knee that was peeking out through my jeans. "Heidi! Did you tear your new jeans?"

"I'm sorry!" I said quickly. "I didn't mean to! I fell off my bike! It was an accident, I swear, and I'm really sorry."

Mom sighed and closed her eyes like she couldn't bear to look at what I'd done to yet another pair of perfectly innocent jeans. "Oh, Heidi. You need to be more careful. It absolutely befuddles me how — well, never mind. Go wash up for dinner."

I fled upstairs, knowing I'd gotten off pretty easy, especially compared to poor Avery.

Maybe I should tell you a bit more about our house. I mean, it's a normal house, but it's full of really not-normal stuff. My dad runs an art auction website, and my mom is the curator of the local art museum, so they both love fancy, expensive, horribly breakable things. Plus, my grandpa is always traveling for his newspaper work, so he keeps bringing us crazy presents like glass bowls from Venice and kangaroo rugs from Australia. My friends say our house is like a museum — everything is exotic or fragile and nothing can be touched. There should be those glass boxes around everything, I swear, and maybe alarms to go off when I get too close, which I do all the time.

Because of me, my parents keep all the nicest things in the room they call the "sala," which is a fancy word for "parlor." They keep that door closed and I'm not allowed to go in there. I usually stay out of Mom and Dad's office, too. And I try to be really, really careful in the living room and the den and the kitchen and pretty much everywhere, although being careful is not something I'm good at.

Basically, the only room where I feel safe is my own bedroom. When I knock things over in there, I don't get in nearly as much trouble. There's a fluffy dark blue carpet so things are less likely to break when I drop them, and the dark color helps to hide the grape juice stains and melted crayons. Mom says I can have a new carpet one day when I'm less clumsy, but I kind of like not having to worry about it.

My walls are light blue like the color of cotton candy (you know, when it's blue instead of pink) and at the top there's a border of dogs playing all the way around. My grandpa and I put that up a couple of years ago, although my mom made lots of big sighing noises about it. I love it so much.

Sometimes I lie on the carpet and just look at all the dogs running and jumping and play-wrestling. I've memorized all the different breeds in the pictures — there are Dalmatians and dachshunds, bulldogs and beagles, Labradors and Lhasa Apsos, Saint Bernards and schnauzers, wheatens and Weimaraners, Pomeranians and pugs and pit bulls and poodles. They always look happy. That's what I want to be like.

There's a blue-and-white-and-green star-pattern quilt on my bed that my aunt Jennifer made for me after the pink poodle blanket disappeared. Of course, it's hard to see the quilt most days because the bed is covered in clothes. I can't ever find anything in the morning, especially whatever it is I want to wear, so I always have to drag out half my closet before I can get dressed.

Really it would be a lot easier if I could just leave it all out there, but Mom wants my room to at least *look* neat every night, so every afternoon I spend, like, half an hour stuffing everything back into drawers or the closet or the giant trunk at the bottom of my bed, knowing it'll all have to come out again the next day.

Oh, I know. I *try* to get organized. Every summer my mom comes through and shows me how to fold everything and arrange it by color and hang my shoes in the racks on the back of the closet door, but I can't keep it like that! I don't have time! People who can do that are the ones who are "mystifying," if you ask me. Don't they have homework and books to read and soccer practice and other people's dogs to hang out with?

I dropped my backpack beside the door and dug through the clothes on my bed until I found a pair of old black pants and a dark green shirt to change into. Then I scooped up a pile of clothes in my arms and stuffed them all into the first open drawer. The ones that didn't fit in there went into the trunk, which is this enormous old chest we found up in my other grandparents' attic. It was supposed to be a place I could dump all my toys and puzzles and games to get them off the floor, but it kind of turned into a trunk full of everything that didn't have somewhere else to go. I crammed my clothes on top and sat on the trunk so it would close.

A car door slammed outside. Dad was home!

"WOOF! WOOF! WOOF!"

I froze. Somebody was barking very close by . . . and it wasn't hard to guess who.

CHAPTER 5

I hurtled out of my room and raced down the stairs. My feet slipped on the fancy silk Persian carpet in the den and I stumbled forward into the kitchen, trying not to fall but, of course, my feet went one way and I went the other and I basically nearly catapulted myself into the salad Mom was making, but luckily Dad caught me just in the nick of time.

"Heidi bear!" he said, giving me a big bear hug as if I had just thrown myself into his arms on purpose. Mom wasn't fooled, but she rolled her eyes and didn't say anything.

"Hi Daddy!" I said, talking fast and loud to drown out the barking outside. "How was your day? Was it great? I bet it was great and you sold lots of famous old stuff hey you know what's on TV tonight that really funny sitcom with the cool lady with the glasses did you remember to record it I bet you didn't you'd better go check don't you think?"

"Heidi, good gracious, let him take off his coat," Mom said. "And use your inside voice, please."

"Calm down," Dad said, patting my head. "Who hit fast-forward on the Heidi remote?"

A big, furry, very loud dog named Yeti, I thought.

Mom tilted her head. Uh-oh. "Do you hear barking?" she asked.

"NO!" I shouted. They both gave me a funny look. "I mean, that'd be cool, if you did, but I don't, oh well, too bad," I said, trying to fiddle with things on the counter so I looked all casual. My mom carefully moved her cell phone and a crystal fruit bowl out of my reach.

"I heard it, too," Dad said, "as I got out of the car. Do you think one of the neighbors got a dog?"

"Oh, that must be it," I said fervently. *Please please just believe that.* But Mom had a little thinking wrinkle in the middle of her forehead.

"Who?" she asked. "The Bae girls are allergic to dogs, the Drakes are planning to get kittens, and Ashley and Karen always said they work too much to have a pet."

"There are lots of people on this block, Mom," I said. "It could be anyone."

"Call me crazy," Dad said, "but I kind of thought it was coming from the Lafittes'."

"CRAZY!" I yelled, panicking and flapping my hands around. My mom grabbed the salad dressing out of the way before I knocked it onto the floor, but the pile of mail for Dad scattered everywhere. "Oops," I said. "Sorry." I knelt down to pick it all up.

"What has gotten into you tonight?" Mom said to me.

"Tonight?" I said, still a little too loudly. "Ha-ha! I'm always like this! Ha-ha-ha!"

Mom frowned at me, but Dad laughed. "That's kind of true," he agreed.

"Hmm," Mom said. She knows me way too well, no matter how "befuddling" she says I am. "Well, our lunatic daughter is right about one thing — I doubt Kelly would ever get another dog, after what happened with Snort."

"Stitch," I corrected her, and then cracked up a little at the idea of a dog named Snort.

"Well, it's stopped now," Dad said with a shrug. "I'll go change and be right down."

"Heidi, set the table," Mom said. "If you think you can do that without shouting or flinging any forks out the window." Which was kind of unfair, if you ask me, since the only thing I've ever thrown through a window was a serving spoon and that was because Avery grabbed the back of my chair while I was reaching for the caprese salad and it startled me and I threw up my hands for balance and it just went flying and anyway the window was open and it was totally an accident plus not my fault.

When it's just the three of us, my family eats dinner in the kitchen instead of the dining room. I like the kitchen much better because the dining room carpet is terrifyingly white and the chairs are all covered in this pale damask that is *just begging* for me to drop spaghetti sauce on it. Although I haven't done that yet, I did manage to get a little spot of vinaigrette on the lavender paisley curtains once (don't ask, I have magical destructive powers), and you don't even want to know what a huge disaster that apparently was.

Plus, our kitchen nook has my favorite piece of art in the house (apart from my dog border) on the wall above the table. It's also the least expensive piece of art in the house, but it's one we can all agree on, because it's a map of the world.

My parents love to travel. They always do one big vacation every year. When I was a baby we mostly went to cool places in the U.S. and Canada (like Disney World and the Grand Canyon and the Berkshires). But when I was six we went overseas for the first time, to England, and because I was really well behaved, ever since then I've been allowed to help them plan our trips. So there are pushpins all over the map for where we've been and where we want to go.

The red pushpins are the places my dad has been by himself. The blue ones are where Mom has been, and the purple ones are the places they've been together but without me. Then there are green pushpins for the places we've been all three together, and my favorite, yellow pushpins for the places we really want to go. Plus, my mom let me have some white ones for places I want to go that they've already been, so it kind of looks like there's a purple-white pushpin war going on in Costa Rica and Japan and Iceland.

My parents are totally different people when they're traveling. If we're in another country, they don't care if I spill gelato all over myself or fall off ancient Incan walls or accidentally let all the sheep out of the paddock on a New Zealand sheep farm. They think everything I do is hilarious when we're on vacation. There's nothing expensive for me to break (although I have to admit the Sistine Chapel got off lucky), and we only pack things that we don't mind losing anyway. It's my favorite part of the year.

I set out the knives and forks and water glasses,

thinking about Yeti. Was he cold out there in the shed? It was only October second, and it wasn't too cold outside, plus he had that ridiculous fur coat. But I worried about him anyway. Was he lonely? Did he think I'd abandoned him? Was he super-hungry? Poor dog.

I couldn't really concentrate on what my parents were saying during dinner, because I was thinking about him the whole time.

"Sounds great to me. What do you think, Heidi?" my dad asked.

"What?" I said.

"Space cadet," he said with a smile. "Your mom was saying maybe we should go to India next."

"India!" I said, finally snapping back into the conversation. "Wow! You mean, like, the Taj Mahal and elephants and . . . and . . . Indian food . . . what else do they have in India?"

"Lots of incredible things," Mom said. I glanced up at the map and saw that India had a blue pin in it, so Mom had been there, but Dad hadn't. "You'll love it. We'll definitely ride an elephant. And there are lots of great books set in India. I read one called *Homeless Bird* that was amazing, and I saw another called *The Conch Bearer* that I bet we'd like."

Mom loves to find books we can read together for our trips, set in the place we're going to. We read *The Thief Lord* by Cornelia Funke while we were in Venice and *Under the Mountain* by Maurice Gee while we were in New Zealand, which was really cool.

"And I'll learn to make chicken tikka masala and samosas," Dad said, getting excited.

"You should ask Pradesh's mom for advice," I told him. "She's Ella's piano teacher, and Ella says she makes the best Indian food in the world."

"Great idea," Dad said.

"So we'll do some research and think about it," Mom said. "I just wanted to put the idea out there, since we'd been talking about Asia next."

A couple years ago I said it was unfair that Mom and Dad had been to all the continents (except Antarctica) and I hadn't, so we were fixing that. So far we'd done Peru for South America, Italy and England for Europe, Egypt for Africa, and New Zealand, which we decided counted for Australia. So now if we went to India, that would be all of them (except Antarctica), which I figured would make me pretty much the coolest kid in sixth grade.

After dinner, I finished my homework, and then I went on the Internet in our computer room to see if

I could find any postings about a lost black-and-white Newfoundland. I didn't really know where to look, so it's not surprising that I didn't find anything. Plus, I kept having to close the window really fast every time Mom walked past the door, which she did a lot, probably because she was worried that I'd trip and fall into the computer monitor or accidentally yank the mouse out of its socket or something.

I also double-checked my favorite dog websites to make sure I didn't take Yeti any food that was bad for dogs. I mean, everyone knows that chocolate is really bad for dogs, but did you know that raisins and grapes are totally dangerous for them, too? And there are bad things in onions and garlic as well. I was memorizing the list when my dad knocked on the door and said it was time for bed.

I had to wait *forever* for my parents to go to sleep. I had no idea they stayed up so much longer than me. I could hear them doing the dishes together, and then watching TV and laughing about some online art history course they're both taking. I was really afraid that I'd fall asleep, but I guess I was way too excited and nervous about sneaking out to see Yeti. Plus, it was too weird to fall asleep in regular clothes, which I was still wearing under the covers.

I stared into the dark, trying to name as many

different dog breeds as I could, but I lost count after I got to thirty. Then I tried to match all my friends with dogs in my head, like "If Rory were a dog, what kind would she be?" I think she'd be a Labrador, all action and playing and roughhousing and fun. Kristal would be something graceful and sweet-natured, like a Cavalier King Charles spaniel or a West Highland white terrier, maybe.

Avery would definitely be a Rottweiler. They're big, stocky dogs who look a lot scarier than they really are. I met this really sweet one, Bruno, down the block from Grandpa's house, and he was just a big goofy doofus who wanted to have his belly scratched all day long.

Finally . . . *finally* . . . I heard my parents' footsteps come upstairs. Their bedroom door closed. I was so ready to leap out of bed and run downstairs, but I made myself wait another half hour, until I was pretty sure they were asleep. By then it was nearly *midnight*. Good *grief*, Mom and Dad!

I tiptoed downstairs and went straight to the refrigerator. I found an empty Tupperware container and filled it with sliced ham and a couple of string cheese sticks and some leftover chicken, although I was really careful to make sure there weren't any bones because chicken bones can break and hurt a dog if he tries to eat them. That didn't seem like enough food, so I added the peanut butter sandwich that I was supposed to have for lunch the next day and some leftover brown rice from this experimental healthy dinner my dad had made on Monday.

Then I went out through the garage, where I managed to crash into only two plastic garbage cans and knock over one box of soda bottles for recycling, so really, I'd call that a success.

It was really, really dark outside. Most of the lights were off in all the houses around us. I could see one light still on upstairs across the street, where Ashley and Karen live, and the blue glow of the TV was still flickering from Avery's living room window, which probably meant his mom had fallen asleep in front of the TV.

The gate squeaked a little when I went through it and I stopped for a minute, holding my breath. The only sound was a small curious "woof" from the shed. I hurried over and unlatched the door.

Yeti threw himself into my arms with all the joy of an astronaut finally returning to Earth after, like, three hundred years in space. I had to grab the side of the shed to stop myself from falling over. He danced and jumped around me with his long black-and-white fur swooshing and fluffing. I know some people might disagree, but I'm pretty sure he was just as happy to see me as he was to see the food.

I pulled the door closed behind me and dumped the food out into the second bowl. Yeti licked my hands while I was doing that, like he was saying thank you and also *Quick! Hurry! Out of my way! Let me at it!* As soon as I moved back, he buried his nose in the bowl and ate like he'd never been fed before.

I sat down on the nest of blankets and watched him in the sliver of moonlight that peeked through the dirty window. I wished I could give him a bath. His fur was all clumped with mud and tangled with leaves. I could imagine how that felt.

"Where did you come from?" I whispered to him.

Harrromph chomp chomph roorrfle chomp, he answered, his long black furry jowls wobbling as he scarfed up the chicken.

"I wonder what your owners are like," I said, stroking his side. "I wonder if they know how awesome you are."

Yeti looked up with peanut butter smeared across his nose. His expression was like, *Dude, no one understands how completely awesome I am.* His big pink tongue slurped out, trying to lick the peanut butter off.

I checked the bowl. All the food was gone!

“Ruh-roh,” I said to him. “You’re a big eater, aren’t you?”

Yeti wagged his tail.

“That’s OK,” I said. “I am, too. I’ll bring you more tomorrow before school, if I can.” Oh, man, school . . . I couldn’t leave Yeti in here all day, could I? Surely he needed to be walked. And what if Kelly heard him howling or barking or something? But she’d be gone most of the day, and so would my parents. At least it was Friday.

Yeti nudged my hand with his nose. I’d stopped petting him while I worried about what to do. I went back to rubbing his head and immediately felt better. We’d figure something out. For now, the important thing was being here with Yeti.

The dog flopped down on the blankets beside me and sighed in what I think was a happy way. I lay down next to him with my arm over his back and he licked my nose, which made me giggle.

“I have to go back inside,” I said. “I’m sorry, Yeti. I’ll come back soon.”

Yeti scooted closer to me and rested his head on my other arm. He felt like a giant teddy bear, all soft and snuggly. His long silky ears draped across my wrist and elbow.

"OK," I said, stroking his fur. "Maybe I could stay for a bit longer."

Well, yeah, of course you can guess what happened next. *I fell asleep.* Like the biggest moron on the planet.

When I woke up, there was pale light coming in through the window . . . and the shed door was creaking open.

Busted!

CHAPTER 6

I nearly screamed until I saw it was Avery. He actually did go "AAAAAH!" when he saw me, but it was just a yelp, and then he jumped inside the shed and closed the door behind him.

"Tyler!" he said in a low voice. "What kind of crazy are you?"

"I fell asleep!" I blurted, sitting up. I realized that sometime in the night I must have moved so my head was resting on Yeti like a big furry pillow. The dog raised his head, blinking, and went *rrrroooof* in a low rumbly voice at Avery.

"SHHHHHHH!" Avery hissed at him. "Yeah, I can see you fell asleep, dummy. How long have you been out here?"

"What time is it?" I rubbed my eyes, trying to wake up.

"About six in the morning," Avery said. "My mom is still asleep, so I figured I'd come out and . . . uh . . ."

"You brought him food!" I cried, spotting the dish in his hand. "Avery, you're the best!"

"Oh, blah blah blah," Avery said, turning red as I hugged him. He was carrying a plate with a couple of toaster waffles covered in peanut butter and a few slices of turkey. I scraped the food into Yeti's dish and he went to town on it, eating desperately, as if I hadn't just fed him six hours ago.

"I'd better buy some real dog food today," I said. "He needs proper nutrition." I liked the sound of that. I didn't like it so much when my mom used it to mean we had to eat morc vcgctablcs, but it sounded like a grown-up thing to say about my dog.

"Uh, Earth to Heidi Tyler," Avery said. "That's not your dog. You don't need to buy dog food for him. You need to find his real owners."

"I looked!" I protested. "I checked on the Internet! I couldn't find anything!"

"This is not my problem," Avery said, throwing up his hands. "Unless my mom finds that thing in here, and then I'm going to say I don't know anything about it. Just so you're warned."

"That's OK with me," I said. "I hope he'll be all right while we're at school. Oh my gosh! School! I have to go home! Dad'll be awake any minute!" I scrambled out of the blankets and tripped over the food bowl, landing with a thud and sending up a cloud of dust.

Avery grabbed my hand and hauled me to my feet. "I'm staying home sick today," he muttered, so low I almost didn't hear him. "So I'll, uh, you know . . . let him out."

"You will?" I cried. "That's so amazing!"

"Do *not* hug me again," he said, stepping back before I could throw my arms around him. "Jeez, you cannot get enough of me."

"Thanks so much, Avery!" I said, pulling open the door. He rubbed the short, spiky hair on his head and looked down at the dog. "See you after school — well, after detention, I guess. 'Bye, Yeti!"

Yeti's tail was wagging when I got up, but as I went through the door and started to close it behind me, it slowed to a stop. His head drooped and he looked up at me with deep brown puzzled eyes.

"Sorry, buddy," I said, reaching back inside to pat his head. "I'll be back soon."

He licked my hand and made *the saddest noise ever.* It felt like he dragged my heart right out of my chest. How would I make it through the day, knowing he was back here waiting for me?

But I managed to close the door and hurry across the grass, which was damp and sparkly with morning dew. It was colder than it had been the night before, and I shivered as I went through the gate. Streaks of pale yellow light cut through the thin gray clouds in the sky.

I tiptoed through the garage and slowly, *slowly* snuck the kitchen door open to peek inside.

Dad was in the kitchen! Dad was in the kitchen!

I was doomed. Totally doomed. Beyond doomed. *In big trouble, missy.*

Unless I could sneak by without him noticing me. He had his back to the kitchen door and was slicing bananas for our morning smoothies. Maybe if I timed it just right . . .

Dad dropped the banana slices in the blender and hit the button. As the loud whirring echoed through the kitchen, I slipped through the door and shut it quickly behind me. Keeping my eyes on his back, I edged along the wall, slipped around the doorway into the den . . .

. . . and smashed directly into an enormous metal bird statue that I *swear* had not been there six hours earlier, or in fact *EVER IN THE HISTORY OF MY HOUSE.*

Try to imagine the sound of several washing machines falling down a flight of iron stairs. Now add that to a hailstorm of swords and rakes and pokers, plus, I don't know, a choir of ogres shouting, "LOOK LOOK LOOK, HEIDI IS UP TO NO GOOD!" That's pretty much what that bird statue falling over sounded like to me.

I mean, I *tried* to grab it right away once it started falling, which is how I found out it came in three pieces (at least I hoped to God it was supposed to come in three pieces), since I ended up with an enormous beaked stork head in my arms while a pair of spiky wings knocked me to the ground and a heavy iron torso rolled thunderingly away across the den, ricocheting off the coffee table with a crash and thudding to a stop at the foot of the stairs.

I heard someone yelling with terror, and then I realized it was me and I stopped.

"Heidi?" my dad said from above me. He sounded more puzzled than I thought he ought to, considering he had clearly left this big, sinister, noise-making attack bird waiting here as a trap for me.

My mom came bolting down the stairs, still in her mint green silk pajamas. "What happened? Is everyone — AAAAAAAH! The statue! Mementa's masterpiece!" She clutched her hair (which incidentally was perfect, even though she'd literally just leaped out of bed).

"I'm OK," I said nobly from the floor. "I'm all right. I wasn't impaled by anything."

"The wings!" my mom said frantically. "They're not bent, are they? What about the beak? WHERE IS THE HEAD?"

"I have the head," I said, a little indignant. I couldn't roll over to show it to her because giant spiky wings were still pinning me to the ground.

"It's all right, don't panic," Dad said to Mom. He carefully lifted the wings off me as Mom brought the torso over. They arranged them back together, studying the statue for scratches and cooing over the "delicate interplay" of "planes" and "vortices" or some such gobbledygook.

"No, really, I'm fine," I said, sitting up with the head in my lap. "Everyone stop worrying about me."

"Heidi, what are you even doing up this early?" my mom said. "And isn't that what you wore yesterday? Are you — how did you get covered in dust?" She glanced around, then down at my shoes, and I knew I had to talk fast to keep her from figuring out that I was just coming in.

"Um," I said. Dad took the head from me and balanced it on top of the statue.

"There, it's all right," he said to Mom. "Now at

least we know it'll make the trip to the museum with no problem. Nothing could do more damage to it than Hurricane Heidi."

"Hey," I said, still on the floor. I decided to go with righteous outrage. Maybe that would distract them from the other questions. "That bird wasn't there before! I swear! Plus, it's totally dangerous! I could have poked out an eye! Or been skewered by a beak! That bird statue tried to kill me! You're the ones who brought a dangerous piece of art into the house! There was no way I could avoid running into it!"

"You could have looked where you were going," my mom said, putting her hands on her hips. "You'd be surprised how well that works."

"It's partly my fault," Dad admitted, which was nice and helpful of him. "I brought it up from the basement this morning. I thought the truck would be here to take it to the museum long before our little wrecking ball came downstairs." He lifted me to my feet and checked his watch. "Wait, why *are* you up this early, Heidi?"

"I have school in an hour," I said. "It's not *so* weird that I'm up."

"It *is* so weird that *you* are up," my mom pointed out, and I guess since I normally sleep as late as I can and then have to be poked several times by my parents before I run around in a panic trying to get dressed and out the door at the last second, she sort of had a point.

"Maybe I'm turning over a new leaf," I suggested. "Showering in the morning instead of at night."

"That would be a good idea," Mom said, looking me up and down. "Are your shoes wet? What on earth is all over your shirt?" She leaned toward me, and I had visions of long dark dog hair getting inspected between her perfect fingernails.

"Nothing!" I yelped, jumping back. "I'd better hurry! Showering! And stuff!" I bolted up the stairs before they could say anything else.

Behind me, I heard Dad say, "Wait . . . so why was she dressed *before* showering?" I flung myself into the bathroom and stayed in there as long as possible, so by the time I came out everyone was running around trying to get me and the bird statue out the door, and I was able to zip out to my bike without getting in any more trouble. At least for the moment.

School was *torture*. I mean, I always think it goes by really, really slowly, but that Friday was the *worst*. When I looked at the clock for the fiftieth time and saw that only half an hour had passed, I pulled out my notebook and wrote a note to Ella, who sits right next to me. It was our free reading time, and I'd read my book, *A Dog's Life* by Ann M. Martin, like, three times already.

GUESS WHAT GUESS WHAT GUESS WHAT, I wrote in big letters across the note, and then slid it over to Ella.

She glanced sideways at it, checked that Mr. Peary was at his desk grading papers, and then wrote *What?*

I FOUND A DOG!!!!!!!!!!!!

Ella tilted her head at the note and read it approximately fifty times, as if I'd written it in, like, Russian or something and she had to translate it.

In her tiny neat handwriting, she wrote, *Really?*

I love Ella, but sometimes she needs to work on her enthusiasm.

YES, I wrote. *BEST DOG EVER! Well, him and Trumpet, of course. I LOVE HIM SO MUCH! Hey, can I borrow some dog food? He's a Newfoundland. Do you know what those look like? They're like me! Too big and too crazy. But he's PERFECT. What are you doing after school? Oh, wait, I have detention. How about tomorrow?*

Ella blinked and blinked at the note. She has really pretty sparkly brown eyes and dark curly hair and the best voice anyone at school has ever heard, like, in real life and not on a CD or whatever. Plus, she's been totally amazing about letting me come over and play with Trumpet all the time.

On my other side, Kristal kind of glanced at the note, like she was wondering why I hadn't written it to her, which made me feel a little bad. But she doesn't have a dog, so I figured she wouldn't get as excited as Ella. Only you'd have to be asleep to be less excited than Ella right then. She mostly looked confused.

Why don't you have dog food? she wrote. *Your mom really let you have a dog? A big one?*

"Girls," said Mr. Peary's voice, "that doesn't look like reading."

We both jumped. He raised his eyebrows at us, and we quickly went back to our books. I had to wait until lunch to tell her the rest of the story.

Eric and Rebekah were both taking a makeup math quiz, since they'd missed it when they'd been out of school on Wednesday, so it was just me and Ella and Parker and Danny and Troy and Kristal sitting together at lunch.

"Whoa," Parker said when I flung myself down in the chair next to Danny. "Somebody's got a lot of energy today."

"I think that's her excited look," Kristal said, squinting at me like she was imagining me in a close-up on a movie screen. She took this awesome video class this summer and she's been talking about movies ever since.

"Uh-oh," Danny said, shoving milk cartons and Jell-O cups and raisin boxes out of my reach. "Excited Heidi! Everybody brace yourselves!"

"Ha-ha-ha guess what?" I said all in a rush.

"Heidi got a dog," Ella said, carefully unpacking her brown lunch bag.

"ELLA!" I yelled.

"Oh, I'm sorry," she said. "Was that — I didn't mean to —"

"It's OK," I said, my words tumbling over her words. "I got a dog! Well, sort of, I sort of got a dog, only not really, but I *found* a dog, and he's AMAAAAAAAAAZING, like, the most amazing dog ever in the history of the world."

"You found a dog you actually like?" Danny joked. "What are the chances of that?"

"How did you 'find' a dog?" Troy asked, all detective-like. "Where was it?"

"And isn't your mom having a heart attack about it?" Kristal asked. "How many things has he broken already?"

"Nothing yet," I said. "Well, he hasn't come inside yet. OK, technically, Mom doesn't know about him. But did I mention he's amazing?"

"Heidi," Kristal said, dropping her face into her hands all dramatically. I happen to know that's a move she picked up from her mom.

"Oh, Kristal, please don't tell your mom," I begged. I'd forgotten that they always tell each other everything. "Just give me a couple of days! I'll figure it out!"

"What's to figure out?" Troy asked.

"Your mom will never let you have a dog," Kristal said.

"Especially a big galumphing Newfoundland," Ella said. Kristal kind of gave her a look like, *How do you know so much about it?*, but of course they were both right. I was crazy even to think I could convince her. The last thing Mom and Dad wanted was another, furrier Heidi galloping around the house crashing into priceless bird statues and antique vases.

"Well," I said. "That's what I have to figure out."

"Uh-oh," said Parker.

"Maybe once she meets him," I said. "Maybe once she sees what a good dog he is . . ."

"You sure it's worth it?" Danny asked. "If you're going to beg her for a dog, maybe it'd be easier to get her to say yes to a small one. Like Buttons!" He grinned in a cute goofy way. It was funny because up until two weeks ago he'd been totally against small dogs, but now he was all mushy about his new toy poodle puppy.

"Maybe, but I want Yeti," I said, remembering his soft, thick fur and the way he poked his nose under my hand when I stopped petting him.

"Yeti?" Parker said. "Like Bigfoot?"

"Well, *that's* a bad sign," said Kristal.

"Heidi, where's your lunch?" Ella asked in her quiet, practical way.

"Oh," I said, looking down at the empty table in front of me. "I forgot. I gave it to Yeti last night. That's OK, I'm not hungry."

RRRRRRROOOWWWRRRRRRRRLLL went my stomach. I started laughing, and so did Danny and Ella, who were sitting closest to me and could hear it.

"Here," Ella said, handing me half of her turkey sandwich. Danny gave me his apple juice and half of his cookie, which for some reason made Troy give Danny a really weird eyebrows-wiggling face, but I figured that was just boy stuff and ignored it.

"Thanks, guys," I said. "Anyway, how are your dogs?"

"Oh, we are *so* not done talking about Yeti," said

Parker. "How are you going to take care of him without your parents finding out?"

"And where did he come from?" Troy asked. "Doesn't he have an owner?"

I told them all about finding Yeti in the park, leaving out the bit about how Avery was with me. I got halfway through the story before I realized I'd have to mention Avery's shed. I tried to be like: "So I just hid him overnight," but Troy really wanted to know *exactly where*, and of course when I said, "Um . . . my neighbor's shed," Kristal was immediately like, "You don't mean *Avery*, do you?" And then Ella was like, "Wait, Avery lives next door to you?" and Danny was like, "Whoa, tough break. Can you smell him from your room?" and I was like, "Oh, whatever, don't be mean, and it's not like they use that shed, so they won't care," which I figured was a pretty good way to get around explaining that Avery had said I could use it in the first place.

"Yeeeee," Ella said with a little shiver. "I had no idea I was so close to evil when I came over to your house."

"When were you at Heidi's house?" Kristal asked, poking her mac and cheese with her fork.

"To rehearse for the talent show," Ella said. "I'm so glad we didn't see him! That would have been terrible. Heidi, I'm not sure I'll ever feel safe at your house again."

"So, about my dog," I said, trying to get off the topic of my oh-so-sinister secret friend. "I kind of need to borrow some dog food. And maybe a leash and a collar. Would that be OK, Ella? I could buy one with my allowance that I've been saving, but I'd have to go into town to do that and I won't have time today because of detention after school."

Ella shook her head. "I can loan you dog food, but we only have one leash. And I'm guessing Trumpet's collar would never fit on a Newfoundland."

"I have a spare collar and leash for Merlin," Parker said. "You can have those. But Heidi, maybe you should put up posters or something — you know, 'Is This Your Dog?', that kind of thing."

"I bet Eric's mom might know about a lost Newfoundland," Troy said, whipping out a notebook and scribbling in it. Dr. Lee is a vet. I realized that was a pretty good idea, which made me nervous. I didn't *really* want to find Yeti's owners. But Troy was in mystery-solving mode. "Don't worry, Heidi, we're on the case!" he said, pushing up his glasses.

"Um, OK," I said. "But it's no big deal, you know. . . ."

"Heidi, you're hiding a ginormous dog in Avery's shed so your mom won't find out about it," Kristal said. "Sounds like a big deal to me. Do you even know if it has fleas or anything? It's, like, totally dangerous to make friends with stray dogs."

"Not *this* stray dog," I said, feeling a twinge of guilt. OK, so yeah, Mom has lectured me about saying hi to every dog in the world, and yes, I know you're supposed to be careful, but I hadn't even thought about it with Yeti. He was so clearly perfect and sweet and good.

Fleas hadn't occurred to me, though. Of course, as soon as I thought about it, I started itching everywhere. I scratched my foot under the table, hoping Kristal wouldn't notice.

"Maybe I can bike over and get the leash on my way home," I said to Parker. "That shouldn't make me too late."

"I have a better idea," Danny said. "I'll go get the food and the leash after school, and then I'll bike over to your place and meet you there when you're done with detention. Then I can meet this dog, too. Wouldn't that be awesome?"

"Um," I said, distracted by the crazy eyebrow-waggling that Troy was doing at Parker. "That's really nice of you, Danny." But if Danny and Avery ran into each other . . . well, there'd pretty definitely be trouble. "But —"

"No arguments," Danny said, stealing back part of the cookie he'd given me. "I'll meet you there."

And then the bell rang for the end of lunch, so I really couldn't argue with him.

I tried to tell myself that there was nothing to worry about. Danny would drop off the dog stuff and go, and I'd get to hang out with Yeti all weekend. Only a few more hours and I'd be home with my dog again.

But I had a weird feeling in my stomach. I didn't know what was going to happen, but something told me . . . trouble was coming.

CHAPTER 7

My plan was to go straight over and visit Yeti before I went inside, but when I got home, Dad's car was just pulling into the driveway, so I couldn't escape. I glanced at my wrist, and then remembered that I'd lost my watch a couple weeks earlier — probably at the YMCA pool, but really it could have been anywhere. That was maybe the fourth watch I'd lost already this year. I had a feeling Mom wouldn't be getting me a new one anytime soon, which if you ask me means it's not really my fault when I'm late all the time.

"Hey kiddo," Dad said as he popped out of the car.

"Aren't you home early?" I asked. I glanced over at Avery's yard, but there was no sign of him or Yeti.

"Nice to see you, too," he said. "Your mom and I have that party tonight, remember?"

I wrinkled my nose, trying to remember if I'd heard anything about a party. Every Sunday night, Mom and Dad go over the schedule for the week to make sure we all know who has to be at soccer practice or PTA meetings or whatever, but of course I don't remember it all by Friday night. I mean, that's *days* of keeping something in my brain! I have too much other stuff in there!

"Really?" Dad said as we walked my bike into the garage. "You were so excited about Ashley coming over to babysit."

"Oh," I said. That did sound familiar. "Something about . . . art."

Dad laughed. "Yes, it's a fund-raising gala at the museum. Your mom's been planning it for weeks. It's the opening of the new exhibit for that sculptor Mementa — you may remember *her*."

"Oh, yeah. Her work made a big impression on me," I said, and Dad laughed and laughed. He was still laughing as we came into the kitchen, where Mom was pacing back and forth beside the counter. She was wearing a long shimmery green dress with a pattern of silver feathers that you could only see in the right light. Her hair was down with a little spray of silver feathers pulling it back behind one ear, and she was wearing small emerald earrings and an emerald-and-diamond necklace that matched the color of the dress exactly. She didn't even look like a mom; she looked like a maharani in an Indian fairy tale.

"Wow," Dad and I said at the same time.

Mom actually kind of blushed. "Don't you 'wow' me," she said to Dad. "We're going to be late! Quick, your tuxedo is up on the bed." She whapped his shoulder with her little silver purse. "Quit staring and get dressed, you ninny."

"Ninny," I giggled as Dad hurried off upstairs. "Mom, you look awesome."

"Ah-ah, do not hug me with those hands," Mom said, giving my dirty fingernails a horrified look. "Ashley should be here any minute. We've left money for you guys to get pizza. No horror movies this time, OK? Do I need to call her and tell her that?"

"I *promise*," I said. "We only watched that one because it's British. We didn't know there were going to be so many zombies in it."

My babysitter Ashley says she's an "Anglophile," which means she loves everything about England, like scones and tea and the queen and saying "What what?" and shiny red double-decker buses. At least, that's what I remember from when we went to England; I'm sure she remembers a lot more, since I was only six when we went, but Ashley just went a couple years ago.

She even ended up with a British accent, although it doesn't sound quite like the ones on *Doctor Who*, which we watch a lot when she comes over, because that totally doesn't count as a horror movie, and I think the parts I can understand are funny.

Ashley has a real job during the day at a clothing store in town, which Danny's mom runs. She's a very cool grown-up, at least according to me, because she talks to me like a regular person instead of like I'm just a kid, and also she has spiky blue hair. (Mom said "*absolutely not*" when I asked if I could do that. Although that's probably mostly because she knows I'd get blue hair dye all over the bathroom.)

But would Ashley understand if I told her about Yeti?

A lightbulb went off in my head. While Mom and Dad were out — maybe I could give Yeti a bath! He really needed it . . . especially if I was ever going to introduce him to Mom and Dad. If I took him straight up to my bathroom, and then straight out again . . . what could possibly go wrong?

I know. I seriously said that to myself.

"Mom, I don't really need a babysitter anymore," I said, pulling off my shoes. "I'm practically old enough to babysit other kids now."

Mom stopped checking her BlackBerry and gave me a puzzled look. "I thought you liked Ashley coming over."

"I do!" I said. "Just, you know, if you wanted, it's OK, I don't, like, *need* her here —"

Of course, then the doorbell rang, and I couldn't make Ashley go away once she was already there. That would have been totally rude.

"'Allo, luv," Ashley said, bopping me on the head as she came in. "Look what I've got." She pulled a DVD set out of her big floppy black purse, the one that has ducks all over it. I took the DVDs and read the cover.

"*Robin Hood*?" I said. "I didn't know there was a TV show. I saw the Disney movie — the cartoon where they're foxes. Mom won't let me watch the Kevin Costner one yet."

"This one's much better," Ashley promised. "They've all got proper English accents, and look how spiffing the Robin Hood bloke is." She meant he was cute, and yeah, he really was.

"Hmmm," Mom said, plucking the DVD out of my hands and studying it with a skeptical expression.

"No zombies," Ashley said with a big smile. "Cross my heart."

"All right," Dad called, charging down the stairs in his tuxedo. "Ready to go!"

"Wow, Dad, you look just like James Bond," I said.

"No hugging him either!" Mom said to me. "Oh, *Heidi*, is that apple juice on your shirt?"

"Um," I said, examining the spot she was pointing at, which I had totally not even noticed before. I thought about my mini-lunch. "Probably." *RrrrrrOOOWRRRrrrl* went my stomach again at the thought of food.

"We'd better order that pizza, quick!" Ashley joked.

"Arthur, would you get the Mementa bowls from the garage?" Mom said, checking her makeup in the mirror.

"Ooooh, for the lucky raffle winners," Dad said. He rubbed his hands together as he went out the door.

Suddenly I realized what she'd said and my heart stopped. Bowls! Oh *no*! Was she talking about the ones I'd borrowed for Yeti? Were those supposed to be . . . art?

Well, I guess it was safe to say they weren't supposed to be dog dishes.

We heard some clattering from the garage, and then Dad stuck his head back in. "I don't see them out here, Sarah."

Mom looked confused. "But — of course they are. In a cardboard box, all wrapped up. Check again."

I wanted to sink into the kitchen tiles and disappear. What could I do? Be like, "Oh, *those* bowls? Just hang on a second while I pop over to Avery's, clean out the peanut butter, and get them for you. P.S. Don't mind the dog." I mean, seriously! But was I going to ruin Mom's gala if I didn't?

"Heidi, stop fidgeting," Mom said, snapping her purse shut again. "You'll knock something over." I promptly knocked over a box of crackers and they scattered all over the floor. Mom sighed.

"I'll clean it up!" I said quickly. At least on the floor I could hide my guilty expression.

"I really don't see them, Sarah," Dad said, coming back inside. Oh, man. I was the worst daughter ever.

"Maybe I took them to the museum already," Mom said with a little frown. "That's so odd, I was sure I left them here. Well, we'd better go. We mustn't be late." She straightened Dad's bow tie and he offered her his arm like a gentleman out of a movie.

"'Bye, Mom and Dad!" I called, still picking up crackers. Inside I was in total agony. I *couldn't* confess about the bowls, could I? But I didn't want to destroy their raffle! I didn't know what to do.

"See you in a few hours," Mom said. "Be good! Ashley, we'll be home around eleven, I should think."

"Have fun, kids!" Dad added.

And then, before I could think of a solution, they were gone.

I stood up and dumped the crackers in the trash (or as Ashley would call it, "the rubbish bin"). Now all I had to do was (a) sneak the bowls back into the garage, (b) keep Danny and Avery from running into each other, and (c) slip Yeti into the house, up the stairs, into the bathtub, and back out again without Ashley noticing.

It wasn't as impossible as it sounds. Ashley's a great babysitter, but there's one thing she does that distracts her so much, I could probably burn the house down without her noticing.

I crossed my fingers behind my back and waited hopefully.

Ashley was scanning the pizza menu. "Let's see," she said, "you don't like mushrooms, and I don't like pepperoni . . ."

"Let's just get what we got last time," I said.

"Spinach and ricotta?" Ashley said. I nodded. "Cheers. I'll go ahead and order that. Oh, and then I have to call my mum. You don't mind, do you, Heidi?"

I grinned. "No, that's totally fine. Tell her I say hi!" This was exactly what I was hoping for. Ashley talks to her mom on the phone every day for at least an hour. Usually they start off joking and telling stories, and then by the end they're having a huge shouting fight. But I guess they're not very serious fights because Ashley always calls her again the next day and they're back to happy again.

It's weird, but today it was perfect, because when she's on the phone with her mom she completely forgets about watching me. I could probably sneak fifteen wet Newfoundlands right past her and she'd just keep talking.

As Ashley pulled out her cell phone, I said, "Oh, Danny might come over for a little while. For homework, uh, stuff. So if you hear any noise, that's probably just him. You know, being loud. Because he's a boy. And stuff."

"Oh, right, and *you're* never loud," Ashley teased. She dialed the pizza place number. I waited until she wandered into the kitchen nook, and then I slipped out through the garage. I couldn't wait a minute longer. I felt all warm and smiley just thinking about Yeti.

There was no sign of Avery or his mom as I hurried across their garden. Kelly's car wasn't in the driveway, and only a couple of lights were on. Maybe she was out. In fact, I realized, Mom had probably invited her to the gala. So the coast was clear.

There was a small *hhuuurroof* sound from the shed right before I reached the door, like he heard me coming. I unlatched the door, and Yeti burst out of the shed and threw himself on me. We fell over in a tangle of fur and paws. His tongue slurped up and down my face and his tail wagged and wagged and I put my arms around his big shaggy shoulders and thought that this was probably the best moment of my entire life.

He was *so happy* to see me! Remember what I said about Ella and enthusiasm? Yeti was like a giant shaggy meteor stuffed with enthusiasm. It was the first time I'd ever met someone as excited about something as I was. I wanted to do cartwheels all over the lawn just to let all the happiness inside me loose.

"Jeez," said Avery. His back door banged shut behind him. "You guys look like idiots."

"Aww, are we idiots?" I said to Yeti in a mushy voice, hugging his big shaggy head. "Are you the handsomest guy? How was your day? Were you good?" He poked his nose in the crook of my neck and I wriggled away from him, giggling.

"He was fine," Avery said, crossing his arms and slouching against the wall of his house. "Hey, Mom called the school and made sure they're going to give me an extra day of detention, since I missed it today. Wasn't that thoughtful of her?"

"Oh, Kelly," I said. There was nothing I could say about Avery's mom. I didn't get why she was so nice to me and so mean to Avery. Sometimes I don't even understand why my mom is such good friends with her. Although if you ask my mom, everything that went wrong with that family is Avery's dad's fault.

I rolled away from Yeti's big white paws and stood up, brushing grass off my jeans. He capered around me, poking me with his nose and dancing and jumping. He couldn't take his eyes off me. I felt the same way. I buried my hands in his fur, grinning at him.

"Did your mom go to my mom's gala?" I asked Avery.

"Yeah," he said. "All dressed up. I asked her what I was supposed to do for dinner, and she said I wasn't an infant, I ought to be able to feed myself. So after she left, I cracked all the eggs in the fridge and poured the rest of her special soy milk down the drain."

"No way!" I said. "Avery! Are you serious?"

"What?" he said. "She was asking for it."

I looked down at Yeti and shook my head. "You're going to get in so much trouble, Avery." The dog looked back at me like, *Can you believe some people?*

He shrugged. "Maybe the eggs cracked in the shopping bag. She won't know. Anyway, I don't care."

I didn't believe that, but I didn't want to argue with him. "Just come over and have pizza with us," I said. "After Ashley gets off the phone. So guess what? I had the best idea!"

"Uh-oh," Avery said, rolling his eyes.

"Mom and Dad will be gone for hours," I said, "so I'm going to take Yeti inside and give him a bath!"

"That is not the best idea," Avery said, shoving his hands in his pockets. "That is the opposite of the best idea."

Yeti sat down next to me and I crouched to hug him, picking twigs out of his black-and-white fur. "It *is* the best idea," I insisted. "We can wash him in my bathtub and then bring him back outside. Ashley won't even notice. He totally needs a bath, look at him. Besides, don't you think Mom will like him better if he's all cleaned up before she meets him?" I smiled brightly at Avery.

"You are a crazy person, Tyler," said Avery. "And none of this *we* business. Leave me out of it."

Right then, I heard a *cling-cling* from our driveway. Danny peeled up to our house, wobbling on his bike from the weight of the bag hanging from one of the handlebars.

Whoops. So much for keeping Danny and Avery apart. A ferocious scowl was already spreading across Avery's face like an oncoming thunderstorm.

"Hey Heidi!" Danny called, leaning his bike against our garage.

"What's *he* doing here?" Avery growled.

"He's helping," I said.

Danny came through the gate, and Yeti bounded right over to him, wagging his tail. All of Yeti's fur rippled when he moved, like waterfalls flowing off his back. Danny went "Heeeeyy!" and held out his hand for Yeti to sniff. Yeti bumped his fingers, pushing them up onto his head so Danny could pet him.

"Oh, man!" Danny said. "He's totally awesome! Buttons will love him!"

Avery snorted. "Buttons. That's the stupidest name for a dog I've ever heard."

Danny noticed Avery for the first time. He frowned, too, rubbing his free hand through his dark hair. "Heidi, is this jerk bothering you?"

"No!" I said quickly. Avery looked mad enough to break something. "He's helping! Well, he was helping. But I'm about to give Yeti a bath, so I guess Avery's going back inside. Right, Avery? You don't want anything to do with it, right?"

"I can help you with that," Danny said, standing up and looking all important, like helping me give a dog a bath was the most heroic thing he'd do all day.

"Forget it," Avery said. He glared at Danny. "I'm helping with the stupid dog's bath. You can run along home."

"*You* go home," Danny said. "Heidi and I don't need your help."

"I'm already home, stupid," Avery said. "And Heidi and I were doing fine with Yeti until *you* came along."

"Oh my gosh, enough," I said, exasperated. "Listen, right now I am taking Yeti inside and giving him a bath, and I don't care if you both want to come hold down a wet dog for me or if I have to do it myself, but I don't want to hear any more arguing about it. OK?"

"Well, I'm coming," Danny said, folding his arms.

"Me too," Avery said grouchily.

Great. Nothing could go wrong with this plan.

CHAPTER 8

"All right," I said, taking a deep breath. "Avery, go get the bowls from the shed."

"Why?" he said, like he was ready to pick a fight.

"Because I have to put them back in the garage!" I said. "Are you going to help or not?"

Avery stomped over to the shed and slammed the door open. As he vanished inside, Danny whispered, "I can make him go away if you want. You must be so sick of him."

"No, it's fine," I said. I knew Danny was probably confused, but I didn't want to give him a long explanation about Avery right then. "Did you bring a leash?"

The collar he'd brought from Parker's was deep purple, as wide as a ruler, and just barely fit around Yeti's neck with room enough for him to breathe. Yeti squirmed and twisted his head around trying to see what I was doing, but I finally snapped it on and clipped the long black leash onto the silver loop. Yeti immediately tried to grab the leash in his mouth.

"No," I said firmly, taking it away.

He wagged his tail and gave me a look like, *Oh, I can wait. I WILL be the boss of this leash!*

"Here," Avery said, stomping up and shoving the bowls at me. Danny grabbed Yeti's leash while I juggled the two Mementa "masterworks." They were covered with dog hair and bits of peanut butter, but I have to say, even if they hadn't been, they still didn't look like art to me. If one of them crawled out from under my bed, I'd probably scream and throw my alarm clock at it. They were *ugly*. But I had to clean them and put them back in the garage, and then hope my dad would just think he missed them.

Yeti was jumping around at the end of his leash, trying to grab it in his mouth and wrestle it away from Danny.

"Whoa buddy," Danny said, skidding across the lawn. He wrapped the leash more firmly around his hand. "Calm down! Man, he must weigh like twenty times as much as Buttons does."

"I can take him," Avery said. "I'm stronger than you. And you're doing it wrong."

"I *am not*," Danny said just as Yeti lunged toward the fence and nearly yanked Danny off his feet.

"Come on, let's go," I said before they could start fighting again.

Yeti dragged Danny through the gate and up the driveway. He would have kept going to the street, but then he saw me open the side door in the garage and he came bounding back with Danny flailing along behind him.

I rinsed the bowls under the water tap and dried them with one of the blankets in the garage, then packed them back into the cardboard box. Yeti sniffed through the other boxes while I did that. Danny watched him warily, waiting for him to lunge away again, while Avery watched Danny.

As I tucked the bowl box carefully behind a pile of other boxes, Yeti stuck his nose into a bag of birdseed. His tail went *wag wag wag* as he poked his head to one side, then the other, burying his nose farther inside the bag. Suddenly he jumped back and sneezed enormously: *KRRRCHOOOOOF! KRRRCHOOOOOOF! KKRRRRRRSNOOOOOOOOOOOOOOOFT!*

The bag tipped over. Birdseed exploded in all directions, across the floor and through the air as Yeti shook himself. Startled, Yeti leaped sideways, crashed into a wall of boxes, and knocked over a whole file of art museum fliers.

"Ack!" I yelped as the papers scattered under my feet.

"See, you're doing it wrong!" Avery shouted, trying to grab the leash from Danny. Yeti started barking with alarm as the boys tugged the leash back and forth.

"Shhhhhh!" I said. I shoved myself between Avery and Danny and knelt beside Yeti. He stopped barking, wagged his tail, and licked my face. "Good boy, Yeti," I said. "Shhhhh."

"Good boy?" Avery said indignantly. "Look at the mess he made!"

"It's OK," I said, although it was kind of a disaster. "I'll clean it up later. But we have to keep him quiet. Even Ashley might get suspicious if she hears barking from inside the house!"

Danny laughed. I pried the leash out of their fingers and hung onto it myself. *Boys*, I thought. *More trouble than they're worth.*

"All right, now quietly," I said. "Ashley's probably in the nook, so we just have to sneak past. *Quietly.* Ready?"

They both nodded. I led Yeti over to the kitchen door and carefully opened it a crack.

Ashley was sitting at our kitchen table with her back to the door.

"I know!" she said. "It's barmy! That's what I said! You're off your nut! That doesn't taste like popcorn at all! And then you'll never guess what *she* said!"

She was laughing, which meant she was still in the early stages of the phone call. Yeti poked the door with his nose and it swung open a few more inches. I wrapped the leash firmly around my hand and waved to the guys.

Cautiously we tiptoed around the doorway and into the den. This time I kept an eye out for menacing bird statues, but nothing had appeared in the last ten minutes.

"And *then* she goes, 'I *do so* look like Keira Knightley!' Imagine!" Ashley's voice floated out of the kitchen behind us.

Yeti's nose was going nuts, like it was on a little motor of its own. He leaned away from me like he wanted to go explore, but I used the leash to keep him close to my side as we hurried through the den. I could still hear Ashley laughing as all four of us galloped up the stairs.

As we reached the upstairs hallway, Yeti nearly lunged away from me, but Danny threw himself in the way and I was able to steer the big dog into my bathroom, which is across the hall from my room.

"Is that your room?" Danny said, glancing through my open door. He started laughing at the giant piles of stuff that covered the carpet and the bed. "That's hilarious. It's just like your locker! How do you ever find anything?"

I laughed, too. "Well, it takes a while," I admitted. "But come on, I bet your room isn't any better."

"OK, yeah. You got me there," he said.

"Yeah," Avery said, peering into my room as well. "Heidi's room is always like that."

Danny gave Avery the weirdest look, as if a second head had just popped out of Avery's elbow and announced that he was my best friend. Avery stared back at him like he was daring him to argue.

"OK, into the bathtub!" I said brightly. I could ignore the weirdness; oh, yes, I could.

But pretending everything was normal with Avery and Danny turned out to be the easy part, compared to getting Yeti into the bathtub. As soon as he spotted the tub, the Newfie dug his paws into the fluffy sky-blue bath mat and tried to scrabble backward out of the room. We piled inside and shut the door so he couldn't go anywhere. He went *rooooooooor* in a disgruntled way and buried his head behind my knees.

"Come on, Yeti!" I said, trying to sound cheerful and encouraging. I unclipped his leash, hooked my fingers through his collar, and tugged him toward the tub. "This'll be fun! A bath! Oh, boy!"

"Oh, *brother*," Avery said as Yeti wriggled loose and tried to hide behind the toilet. He managed to fit his head between the seat and the wall, but of course the rest of him was way too big to squeeze in anywhere. I wrapped my arms around his chest and tried to heave him into the tub. I swear he must have weighed twice as much as I did.

Danny was laughing again, almost hard enough to fall over. Even Avery had stopped scowling and looked like he was trying not to crack up.

"I'm glad you're so amused!" I said to Danny. "Now could you PLEASE HELP?"

"Here," Avery said, tucking the shower curtain up on the rod so it was out of the way. Yeah, even my shower curtain has dogs on it. It's white with little black dogs chasing yellow rubber ducks through a bunch of blue and green squares. Well, I think it's pretty cute, anyway. And it matches the dark blue walls and white tiles and my bright yellow toothbrush.

"What do you want me to do?" Danny said. "Are we going to lift him in? For real?"

I tried to think what the trainers on my favorite dog shows would do. "Oh!" I said. "Did Ella give you any treats? Maybe that would help." Yeti lifted his head and peeked out at me when I said "treats." That seemed like a good sign.

While Danny unzipped his backpack, Avery turned on the tap and felt the water coming out of the faucet. "Is this warm enough?" he asked me as the tub started to fill up.

I leaned over and felt it. I didn't really know the exact right temperature it should be, but I figured as long as it wasn't too cold or too hot it would probably be OK.

"Yeah, sure," I said, just as Danny pulled a dog biscuit out of his bag and held it out to Yeti.

Yeti's eyes lit up. He practically did a backflip with a triple somersault to get to the biscuit. Before I could even turn around, he had snarfed the treat out of Danny's hand and leaped right over me into the tub.

Splash!

Water soaked my arms and splashed over the side onto my jeans. Avery and Danny both jumped back out of the way.

"Oh, very helpful, thanks, guys," I said, wringing out the bottom of my shirt. "Danny, hand me another treat."

Yeti had his nose in the water, lapping it up, but he looked up when I held out the biscuit and splashed over to me. He sat down right there in the tub and snarfed it up, *crunch crunch crunch.* His ears swung and flapped on either side of his huge head. His long pink tongue licked the last crumbs out of my fingers and then he sat there, panting. He looked very pleased with himself.

The water was slowly rising up to his stomach. Mud was caked through his fur all along his underbelly and legs.

"Danny, check under the sink," I said. "There should be a bottle of baby shampoo under there." I knew you weren't supposed to use regular human shampoo on a dog, but I'd read online that if you didn't have dog shampoo, you could use really mild baby shampoo.

Danny pulled out a light pink bottle and handed it to me.

"Uh, why do you have *baby* shampoo?" Avery asked. "Like, you can't wash your hair without crying, or what?"

"Shut up, Avery," Danny said.

"It's from when Julia visited," I said, squirting some of it into my hand.

"Oh," Avery said. "Her cousin," he added to Danny. "She's two." Avery's face was like, *See? I know a lot more than you do.* Danny wrinkled his forehead like nothing made any sense. He sat down on the edge of the bathtub beside me and watched as I rubbed shampoo along Yeti's legs.

Now that Yeti was in the tub, he seemed a lot calmer. He sniffed my hands while I worked my fingers through his thick black-and-white fur. He tilted his head while I poured water over his back. I was really careful not to get any water in his ears. I used one of my own washcloths to wash his face so his ears would be safe.

Yeti thought that was pretty hilarious. He snagged the washcloth right out of my hand as I was rubbing under his chin. He shook it and shook it like he was defeating a wild animal and then dropped it in the tub and gave me a satisfied *so there* expression.

"Yes, you're very clever," I said to him, scratching his chin. I searched through his fur carefully, remembering what Kristal had said about fleas, but I didn't see anything. Muddy water poured off Yeti's legs as I rinsed him off. We had to empty the bath and run it again twice. I gave Yeti a few more biscuits to keep him calm, but he didn't seem too worried.

"I can't believe your babysitter isn't wondering what you're doing," Danny said.

"She's definitely going to want to know why you're all wet," Avery said. He was leaning against the door with his arms folded.

"I'm not *that* wet," I said, and Yeti picked that exact moment to stand up and go *SHAKE SHAKE SHAKE SHAKE SHAKE SHAKE SHAKE.* I shrieked as he splattered water all over me. Danny jumped up with a yell, but there wasn't anywhere to escape to. Even Avery got pretty splashed, over by the door. Tiny muddy droplets speckled the walls and tub. Yet another thing I'd have to clean up before Mom and Dad got home.

Pant pant grin, went Yeti.

"You were planning that all along, weren't you, you silly dog?" I said to him. He tilted his head like, *Who, me? This innocent face?*

"Blargh," Danny said, wiping his face with his hands.

Avery snickered, but he stopped smiling quickly when Danny looked over at him.

"Can I use your towel?" Danny asked me. My

fluffy blue towel, the same cheerful color as the bath mat, was hanging next to him.

I smacked my forehead. "I totally forgot! We need a towel for Yeti!"

"Just use yours," Avery suggested snidely. "I'm sure he doesn't smell any worse than you do."

"Hey." Danny bristled.

"Ha-ha," I said, "but if Mom sees muddy paw prints on my towel, I'll be in *real* trouble." I could just imagine the look on her face. Hiding a dog in a shed and feeding him out of priceless art was one thing. Getting my towel dirty to clean him was *quite* another. "No, we need to get one of the old towels from the linen closet."

"I'll get it," Danny said, stepping toward the door.

"No, *I'll* go," Avery said. "I know where it is." He gave Danny a *so there* face that looked a lot like Yeti's. And then he squeezed quickly out the door and shut it behind him.

Danny turned to me and put his hands on his hips. "OK," he said. "I don't get it. How come Avery knows your house so well? And your cousin and everything?"

Well, I didn't care if he knew. It was only Avery who was weird about being friends with me. And

I figured it was kind of too late to keep it a secret anymore.

I shrugged. "We've known each other forever," I said.

"But you're not, like . . . *friends* with him, are you?" Danny asked.

"Yeah, I am," I said just as the bathroom door opened again. "So what?"

Danny looked flummoxed. He stood there staring at us as Avery came through the door holding a faded old green towel. Meanwhile, Avery was looking at me, and I was looking at the towel, so none of us was looking at Yeti.

And that's when he made his great escape.

CHAPTER 9

"YAAAAAAAAAAAAAAAAAAAH!" I shrieked as a giant wet ball of fur blasted past me. Avery lunged to stop him, but Yeti slipped right through his hands. I wasn't even on my feet yet when I heard an enormous *CRASH!* from down the hall.

"Oh, no!" I yelled. "No! Yeti! No!" I pushed past Danny and Avery and we all ran down the hall to Mom and Dad's room. One of their matching white china bedside lamps was lying on the floor in pieces. And in the middle of their perfect lavender comforter was a huge wet dog.

Yeti was rolling and rolling and scrunching himself across the bed, burying his nose under the pillows and flinging them up in the air again. Long black and white dog hairs trailed across the covers behind him. He kicked his paws in the air and rolled around on his back, making happy *rruuuff*ing noises while his shaggy ears flopped around his head.

"Yeti!" I cried, horrified. "Stop! Off!"

Yeti surged to his paws and blinked at me. He was standing right in the center of Mom and Dad's bed.

"WOOF," he declared like, *I claim this bed for the kingdom of Yeti.*

"Get *off*," I said, climbing on the bed to grab his collar.

Yeti was having none of that. As soon as I reached for him, he sprang off the bed, barreled right through Danny's and Avery's outstretched hands, and galloped away down the stairs.

"You guys!" I cried. "Be more helpful!"

"I'm sorry!" Danny sputtered.

"We'll get him!" Avery said, spinning to run downstairs.

"AAAAIIIIIIIEEEEEEEEEEEEEEEEEEEEEEEEEEEEE!!!!!!!!!!!!!!!!!!!!!!!!!!!!!!!!"

CRASH!

"Uh-oh," I said.

"I think Ashley's noticed the dog," Avery said.

CRASH! BAM BAM BAM! CRASH CRASH!

"A BEAR!" Ashley screamed. "THERE'S A BEAR IN THE HOUSE! IT'S KNOCKING OVER THE ART! IT'S TEARING DOWN THE CURTAINS! MOM, I HAVE TO CALL YOU BACK!"

We ran down the stairs just in time to see a black-and-white blur skid by on the Persian carpet and slalom into the living room. I jumped down the last couple of stairs and crashed into Ashley, running toward us from the kitchen.

"Did you see that?" she said, panting. "There's a giant beast in the house! I don't know how it got in!"

"Me neither!" said Danny from behind me.

"Never seen it before," Avery added quickly.

"That's so weird," Danny said, looking innocent.

"It is *not* a giant beast," I said, giving the boys a dirty look. "That's my *dog*."

"Your —" Ashley's mouth opened and closed, but no sounds came out.

CRASH!

"Don't just stand there!" I shouted at Danny and Avery. "Go through the kitchen and chase him back this way!"

They ran off through the den into the kitchen. Our house loops around the central staircase, with the den and the kitchen and the garage on one side and the living room, sala, and office on the other side. I ran into the living room, hoping we could corner Yeti if we came at him from either side.

The first thing I saw was that the sala door was still closed, which made me breathe a sigh of relief.

All the fanciest, most expensive stuff is in there, with the piano, where I can't do it any harm. But the living room also has a lot of horribly fragile stuff, and my heart sank as I saw tiny green-and-gold fragments of something scattered across the thick white rug.

Yeti was sitting on the couch, blinking sweetly and looking as if he really had no idea why there were shattered pieces of a porcelain vase all over the floor. I recognized that vase. I'd been tiptoeing around it ever since Mom bought it at one of those upscale flea markets she always goes to. It used to sit on a side table next to the couch. Now . . . not so much.

If you ask me, it wasn't a very pretty vase anyway. But I had a feeling Mom might not see it that way.

Yeti buried his nose in the pale green throw pillows and started rolling. He flopped onto his side and gave me a look that said *Come on! Come play with me! I call this game Wet Dog on a White Couch! So much fun!*

"It *is* a dog!" Ashley said in a hushed voice behind me. "Do your parents know about this?"

"Uh . . . not exactly," I said. "I mean, not yet. But they will! I just have to introduce them the right way."

"Well, you're off to a great start," Ashley said, rolling her eyes.

Danny tiptoed out of the kitchen and started to

sneak up behind the couch. I moved slowly forward, reaching out to the dog.

"Hey, Yeti," I said, trying really hard to sound calm. "Hey, good boy. Don't you want to go back outside? Wouldn't that be a great idea? Yes, you do, I know you do, good boy." He was still flopped over, watching me sideways, and his tail was thumping against the arm of the couch.

As I took a step closer, he grabbed the forest green chenille blanket from the back of the couch in his jaws and yanked it over on top of him. With a delighted *grrrruff* he started shaking it and digging into it with his paws. I flinched as his claws snagged on the delicate loops of wool.

"AHA!" Danny yelled suddenly, hurtling over the back of the couch. But as he jumped, his foot slipped on the rug. Also, the triumphant yell kind of gave him away. By the time he landed on the couch, Yeti had launched himself off the cushions and was running around the room barking. His tail swished dangerously close to several expensively framed photos of my family in exotic places.

"WOOF! WOOF! WOOF! WOOF!" Yeti barked delightedly.

"Stop him!" Ashley shrieked. "The curtains!" Our living room curtains are long and drape elegantly all the way to the floor, which makes them really easy to get tangled up in, as I happen to know from personal experience.

Danny threw himself off the couch and tried to block the way to the curtains. I ran around the other side of the couch, but Yeti was already galloping to the kitchen door. He knocked over a chair and then skidded to a stop as Avery burst out of the kitchen. With another woof of excitement, Yeti whipped around and dashed back toward Ashley.

"EEEEEEEEEEEEEEEEEEEEEEEEEEE!" she shrieked. Her blue hair was practically standing on end. She covered her eyes with her hands. "It's the Hound of the bloody Baskervilles!"

"He won't hurt you!" I cried, but Ashley had already flung herself to the floor. Yeti bounded right over her and out of the room. I could hear his massive paws pounding up the stairs again.

"That dog is *insane*," Danny panted, flopping against the arm of the couch.

"He's just excited!" I said. "He probably thinks this is a wonderful game. Maybe nobody's ever played with him before."

I looked around at the catastrophe Yeti had left behind. This would take *forever* to clean up . . . plus I'd have to explain how so many things got broken. I hadn't even seen what he'd done in the kitchen and den yet. "Danny, give me another treat," I said. "I'll go get him."

"You're lucky your parents won't be home for a while," Ashley said, patting her forehead with her sleeve. "Oh, Heidi, this is chaos."

"I'm sorry," I said, taking a biscuit from Danny's outstretched hand. "I'll clean it up, I pro —"

Slam.

We all jumped. Was that a car door?

"That didn't come from upstairs," said Avery.

"That came from *outside*," said Danny. He looked terrified.

"I'm sure it's just the pizza," I said. My heart was pounding. "Right, Ashley?"

Ashley was peeking out the curtains of the living room. Her face went pale.

"It's your parents," she said. "They're home early!"

CHAPTER 10

We're dead!" Danny yelled. "They're going to kill us!"

"We have to hide Yeti!" I said frantically.

"And me!" Avery said. "They'll tell my mom! She'll ground me forever! Hide *me*!"

"Me too!" Danny said. They both looked around like they were thinking about diving under the couch.

"Quick, upstairs!" I said. The boys both ran past me and charged up the stairs. I glanced out the window beside Ashley and saw my parents hurrying up the walk to the front door. They'd left the car in the driveway — so maybe they were only coming back to get something. Maybe they'd leave again without noticing the mess.

Yeah, and maybe pink schnauzers would fly out of my ears.

"Please don't tell them about Yeti!" I said to Ashley. "I want to tell them myself, I promise I will, just not yet. Just distract them until they go away!"

"Heidi!" Ashley cried. "How am I supposed to do that?"

"I don't know! Tell them the broken stuff is my fault! They'll believe that." I turned and ran up the stairs. I threw myself into my bedroom just as I heard the keys turn in the front door.

"Why, *helloooo*!" Ashley blurted in a too-loud, too-cheerful voice. "Fancy seeing *you* home so early!"

I closed my door behind me. Danny was running around my room looking for a place to hide. Avery had buried his head in his hands. Yeti was the only one who looked calm. He was sprawled across my bed with an extremely contented expression.

"Yeti, come!" I said. He jumped off the bed and trotted over to me, wagging his tail. I hooked my fingers in his collar and led him over to the closet, hoping I could hide him in there.

But the closet was full of boxes of my old toys and piles of clothes and shoes. There was no way Yeti would fit in there as well. And neither would the boys.

"Heidi?" I heard my mom's voice call from downstairs. Danny gave me a panicked look.

"Under the bed!" I said. "Both of you! Quick!"

"I'm not hiding under there with him!" Avery protested.

"Yeah, same!" Danny agreed.

"Fine, then you can explain to my mom what you're doing here with this dog!" I said, exasperated.

They dove to the floor and scrambled under the bed. Yeti leaned against my hand and looked up at me trustingly.

"I'm sorry, Yeti," I said. "But we have to hide you somewhere." I looked around, my heart pounding. There was only one option.

I threw open the chest and flung everything out of it onto the floor. Stuffed dogs bounced and rolled across the carpet. Yellow rain boots landed on striped sweaters. I discovered that I had way more socks with no matches than I'd realized. I heaved the last pile of shirts out of the bottom and pointed to the chest.

"Yeti, in!" I said. The dog stared at the trunk, then looked at me like, *You can't be serious.*

Thump thump thump. Footsteps on the stairs!

I waved the biscuit in Yeti's face. "Quick!" I said. "Get in!"

He looked at the chest doubtfully, and then he shook himself so all his fur fluffed out and jumped right in. I gave him the biscuit and he flopped down. Quickly I stuffed a couple of shirts along the top edge to leave a gap. I closed the lid and leaped onto my bed just as my door flew open.

"Heidi?" my dad said. "What's going on? Did I hear voices in here?"

"Nope," I said. I nearly had a heart attack as I spotted the bottom of Danny's foot sticking out from under my bed. Dad was looking around the room with a confused expression. Carefully I sidled sideways and kicked Danny's foot. It vanished quickly.

"What are you guys doing home?" I said. "Wasn't the party fun? Do you need to go back? You probably need to hurry back, well, it was great to see you, have fun —"

"We came back to find those bowls for the raffle," Dad said. "I really thought I heard something. . . ."

"Did you check the garage?" I said quickly. "Maybe you should check there again. Maybe behind something. Maybe you just missed it. I bet that's it."

"That's where your mom is looking," Dad said. Hope flooded through me. If Mom was in the garage, maybe she wouldn't even come back inside — maybe she wouldn't see the mess —

Ooorrrrroooorrrrrorrooorrooo.

A muffled whimper came from the chest.

Dad blinked. And blinked some more. "Did you —"

"Ooooooorrrrooooooo," I said, clutching my stomach. "Did you hear that? Man, I am *so* hungry."

"HEIDI!" my mom bellowed from downstairs. "GET DOWN HERE THIS MINUTE!"

Uh-oh. I was definitely in trouble now. On the other hand, at least it would get Dad out of my room.

But just as I stood up, the worst possible thing happened.

The doorbell rang.

Ding-dong!

Immediately the chest went, "ROWRF ROWRF ROWRF ROWRF ROWRF!"

If it hadn't been so terrible, I would have laughed at the expression on my dad's face. He looked as surprised as if a giraffe had just poked its head out of my closet.

"Um," I said. "I can explain."

My mom must have flown up the stairs. She was standing behind my dad a heartbeat later. "Did I just hear what I think I heard?" she demanded.

Downstairs I heard Ashley open the door and pay the pizza guy. Of course it was my luck that he'd shown up at exactly the wrong time.

"Heidi," my dad said really slowly. "Is there a *dog* in this room?"

"ROWRF!" the chest announced cheerfully. My mom widened her eyes at it in horror.

"I'm sorry," I said. I lifted the lid of the chest and

Yeti sat up, beaming all over his sweet shaggy face. "Mom, Dad — this is Yeti."

"Oh my," my mom said faintly. "That . . . is a very big dog."

"He's a Newfoundland," I said. "Isn't he wonderful? He's really very good, I swear! He didn't mean to break your green vase."

Mom pressed her hands to her heart. "He broke my green vase?"

Whoops. I guess she hadn't made it into the living room yet.

"It was my fault," I said. My words tumbled over each other. "I just wanted to give him a bath because he was so sad and I thought you would like him better if he was clean but he got away from me and he didn't mean to be bad, he really didn't! He's a good dog — he just doesn't know how big he is! It was an accident! He doesn't mean to make a mess. He just wants to be loved. Look how sweet and good he is." I knelt beside Yeti and wrapped my arms around his furry chest. "He's just bigger than he realizes. He wants to be good, he really does."

"Sounds like someone else we know," Dad said, giving my mom a meaningful look.

Yeti went *hrrruff* like he was agreeing with me. He put his front paws up on the side of the chest and hopped over onto the floor. Wagging his tail, he trotted over to my parents to sniff them.

"Oh, no you don't," Mom said, backing up and flapping her silver purse at him. I hurried over and grabbed his collar before he could shed on their nice clothes.

"Where did he come from?" Dad asked.

"I found him," I said. "He was lost and all alone, Dad. He was so sad. He didn't have a collar or anything."

"You *found* him?" Dad echoed. "You don't know who he belongs to or anything?"

"Arthur, we have to get back to the gala," Mom said. "We'll deal with this later."

"Did you find the bowls?" he asked.

"Yes," she said. "They were in the garage, right where I said they were."

"Really?" Dad scratched his head, and I felt a pang of guilt. I had to tell the truth. It was better to confess everything all at once.

"Um," I said. "That was my fault, too. I maybe . . . borrowed them. For a little while."

Mom looked at Yeti, closed her eyes, and put one hand on her forehead. "I don't want to know, do I?" she said.

"I *knew* they weren't there before," Dad said.

"Thanks for being honest, Heidi. I thought I was losing my mind."

"We'll talk to you about this when we get home," Mom said, waving her purse at me. "This is very serious, young lady. I don't know what you were thinking."

"I know," I said. "I promise I'll clean up while you're gone. I'll put new sheets on your bed and everything."

Mom closed her eyes again like the world was too much for her. "It . . . was on our *bed*?"

Oops. "Only for a minute," I said. "Don't worry, it was after his bath so he was very clean and only a little wet. By the time you get back, everything will be all cleaned up. I promise."

Yeti wagged his tail.

"A dog," Mom muttered as she started back down the stairs.

"I told you this would happen eventually," Dad said, following her.

I held my breath until the front door closed behind them.

I couldn't believe it! I guess I'd half expected Mom and Dad to throw Yeti right back out on the streets. At the very least I thought there would be yelling. Well, maybe there'd be yelling later. But for now, I didn't have to stuff Yeti back in Avery's shed. He could stay with me until Mom and Dad came home.

I ruffled his fur. "That wasn't so terrible," I said to Yeti. "No thanks to you and your awesome powers of destruction. Maybe we still have a chance."

"QUIT SHOVING!" Avery hollered from under the bed.

"*You* quit shoving!" Danny grumbled back.

They wriggled out from either side of the bed.

"I thought your mom would be way more mad," Avery said as he got to his feet.

"So did I!" I said. "Maybe she didn't see everything he did."

"You know, I thought *my* house was crazy," Danny said, "but this place is nuts."

I gave them both a big smile. "So . . . who wants pizza?"

"Me!" Danny said.

Avery frowned. "I know that look. This is a trick."

"It's not a trick," I said. "More like . . . a bribe. Free pizza — if you stay and help clean up." I tried flapping my eyelashes at them the way Tara and Natasha do when they want something. "Come on, it'll be fun."

"All right," Danny said. "I can do that."

Avery sighed heavily. "Fine. But only because of the pizza."

CHAPTER 11

Danny and Avery were about as useful at cleaning as they were at catching Yeti. Ashley and I did most of the work while they ate pizza and made rude comments at each other and patted the dog. But I thought the house was looking pretty presentable by the time they left. You'd never know a furry hurricane had blown through.

I walked Yeti outside while Danny got his bike. Avery kicked a stone up and down my driveway until Yeti pounced on it and I had to take it away so he wouldn't eat it.

"Thanks for your help," I said as Danny wheeled his bike toward the street. "And the dog food and leash and stuff."

"Sure," he said, fiddling with his bike chain. "Hey, if you want to bring Yeti to the park tomorrow, I'll probably be there with Rosie and Buttons."

"That would be so awesome!" I said. "I guess it

depends on whether I still have Yeti tomorrow. I don't know what my parents are going to say."

"They'll definitely say no," Avery said, kicking the grass beside the driveway.

"Nice. Thinking positive," I joked, but inside I was pretty worried. "Thanks for your help, too, Avery."

Danny snorted. "Yeah, like letting the dog out of the bathroom."

"That was *your* fault!" Avery flared.

"Oh, stop, it's fine," I said. "Mom and Dad would have found out eventually."

"Yeah, I guess," Danny said. He was still fiddling with his bike chain. He acted like he was waiting for Avery to leave, but Avery was clearly waiting for Danny to leave. Boys are such trouble. I mean, seriously. Well, I wasn't about to stand there all night and wait for one of them to give up.

"All right, good night!" I said, tugging on Yeti's leash. Realizing they were about to be left alone with each other, Danny and Avery both kind of grunted and took off in opposite directions.

I told Ashley I was sorry about a million times, but once she stopped being afraid of Yeti, she thought it was all kind of funny. She helped me find a couple of bowls for Yeti that didn't cost, like, a million dollars each. She even let him lie on the couch in the den with us while we watched the first episode of *Robin Hood*, which was just as good as she'd said it was.

Yeti rested his massive head on my lap with a sleepy contented expression. His eyelids kept drooping, but then he'd suddenly open them again and look up at me, like he was checking that I was still there. I've always thought watching TV would be a million times better with a dog on my lap, and I was totally right. Patting his thick, fluffy fur made me feel calmer and less anxious about what Mom and Dad would say when they finally got home.

I was tired after chasing Yeti around the house, so I went to bed a little early. Yeti trotted up the stairs behind me, and when I climbed into bed, he hopped right up and curled up next to me.

"I should make you sleep on the floor," I mumbled, putting one arm around him. "That's what all the TV dog trainers say." Yeti went *oooooorrrrmmmrrrr* and licked my ear. I giggled. "OK, but don't push me out of bed. All right?"

That plan didn't go so well. I mean, Yeti was *huge*. First, he stole all the blankets, and then I couldn't get my pillow out from under his head, and every time he rolled over it seemed like he was scrunching farther into my space. I kept waking up right before getting dumped out onto the floor.

So I was actually still awake when Mom and Dad came home a little while later. I heard them talking in low murmurs to Ashley and then coming up the stairs. Dad peeked through the doorway into my room.

"Heidi?" he whispered. "You awake?"

I sat up. "Yeah."

He turned on the light as they came in. Mom wrinkled her nose when she saw Yeti curled up on the covers beside me.

"It's OK," I said. "I checked him for fleas when I gave him a bath. He's totally clean!"

Mom and Dad both shuddered. Dad sat on the bed, and Mom pulled up my desk chair and they made me tell them all about finding Yeti. The only thing I left out was the part about accidentally sleeping in the shed. I didn't think Mom would be very thrilled about that.

"He was in Kelly's shed overnight?" Mom said. "Does she know?"

"No!" I said. "Please don't tell her — I don't want to get Avery in trouble."

Mom sighed. She tells Kelly almost everything, but I'm pretty sure she agrees with me that Avery doesn't need any more trouble than he already has.

"I know he's a big dog," I said, running my hand over Yeti's back. "But I really love him and I really want to keep him. Please? Please please? I'll do anything for him. I'll even give up candy." I know Mom thinks I eat too much candy. It's what I spend most of my allowance on (apart from dog biscuits and books). I usually keep my stash in my locker at school so I don't accidentally get chocolate on the couch at home or something dreadful like that.

"Wow," Dad said. "Giving up candy? That does sound serious."

"You did a good job cleaning up downstairs," Mom said. "I appreciate that."

"And in the garage," I said. "And in your bedroom. And in my bathroom. Did you see?"

Mom rubbed her forehead. "You really had a wild time in the half hour we were gone, didn't you?"

"We didn't mean to," I said. "He's really a very good dog. He tries to be good."

Dad held out his hand. Yeti stretched toward him and went *sniff sniff sniff*, and then he licked Dad's fingers like he was saying, *OK, you're all right*.

"Careful you don't get hair on your tuxedo," Mom said. "Heidi, honey, this dog probably belongs to someone. We should try to find his real owners. They must be worried about him."

I shook my head. "Look how thin he is. And he didn't have a collar or anything. I bet they don't care about him at all."

"We'll find out," Dad said. He patted my foot. "Go to sleep, and we'll see what happens in the morning."

All night I dreamed about getting buried in piles of black-and-white fur. A couple times I woke up because Yeti was breathing right in my face. But in the morning when I opened my eyes and saw his big shaggy black ears flopped across my pillow, I felt like I was filling up with happiness like a hot-air balloon.

I buried my face in his neck and he went *huurrrrruff* in a sleepy way.

"Morning, best dog ever," I said, rubbing his stomach. Yeti poked his nose under my pillow, exactly the way I do when I don't want to get up. But then he flipped his head up and sent my pillow flying off the bed. With a small "woof," he rolled over on his back and started wriggling playfully with his paws up in the air. I jumped on him, and we wrestled in the covers until we both fell off the bed with a thump.

"Ow," I said, sitting up and shaking my head. "I wonder if Mom and Dad will let me have a bigger bed. What do you think?" Yeti sneezed and looked surprised. "Yeah, you're probably right," I said. "Let's work on keeping *you* first."

Yeti braced his front paws on the carpet and stretched way, way back like one of my mom's yoga poses. His head went up as we both heard a voice murmuring from the hallway.

I opened my door a crack and listened. I could tell it was my dad on his cell phone, because he always talks louder than he does on the regular house phone. It's like he thinks there's no way someone could possibly hear him on such a tiny thing.

"That's right," he was saying. "Black and white. A Landseer Newfoundland. Really large." He paused for a moment. "No, no collar. The park across from Westminster Elementary." He paused again. "Really? How long ago did they lose him?"

Oh no! My dad couldn't have found Yeti's owner already, could he? That would be so unfair.

Yeti stuck his nose under my hand and gave me a look like, *What? Why are we so worried all of a sudden?*

What could I do? Maybe I should hide Yeti again. If I told Mom and Dad he ran away, I could keep him in Avery's shed and still get to see him every day. Or no — they'd definitely check the shed. Was there anywhere else I could hide him?

Danny's house was way too crowded to hide a big dog; he has three brothers and a sister and they're all loud and a little crazy. Ella's mom wasn't much more of a dog person than my mom, although she'd come around to liking Trumpet by now. Kristal didn't have any dogs, and her mom would call my mom right away if I showed up there trying to hide an enormous Newfoundland.

Maybe Rebekah could help me. She got a new dog over the summer, a tiny Maltese-poodle mix, and I knew her parents loved dogs. I heard my dad wander downstairs, still talking on his cell phone. Quickly I took Yeti's collar and hurried down the hall into our computer room. I shut the door behind me and picked up the phone. Yeti poked his head under the computer desk and began sniffing the cables.

"Don't you dare chew anything," I said to him. "My dad is, like, in love with that computer."

Yeti's face was all *As IF I would do any such thing!* He crouched lower to the carpet and crawled farther under the desk. I dialed Rebekah's number, and she answered after two rings.

"Hello?" she said.

"Rebekah!" I cried. "I need your help! They're going to take away my dog! They're going to give him back to the bad people who don't love him, but *I* love him and I need to keep him and I was thinking maybe we could hide him in your garage oh *no, wait* — your parents are cleaning out the garage this weekend, aren't they? Ack! What do I do? Help!"

"Heidi?" said Rebekah.

"Where else could we put him?" I said. "Does anyone else have a shed or a garage where their parents don't go? He's really big, like, super-huge, like, twice as big as you, but he's the sweetest dog ever and he won't bother anyone and he'll be so good and I don't want him to go back to his terrible owners. . . . Rebekah! What do I do?"

"What?" said Rebekah. "What dog? What are you talking about?"

"Yeti!" I said. "Remember? Yeti!"

"Yeti?" she echoed. "Like Bigfoot? You have a Bigfoot?"

"Did I wake you up or something?" I asked. Then I remembered that she hadn't been with us at lunch when I told everyone about Yeti.

"I was just making sandwiches," Rebekah said. "I'm going to the park today. You'll never guess with who."

"Heidi!" my mom called from downstairs.

"OH, NO!" I yelped. "They're coming! They're going to take him away! Rebekah, we're doomed! Poor Yeti! It's the end of the world!"

"I'm sorry," Rebekah said, and she sounded like she meant it, although she clearly had no idea what I was talking about. "Anyway, don't you want to guess?"

"HEIDI!" my mom yelled again.

"I gotta go," I said, throwing my free hand up in despair. Obviously Rebekah was going to be no help.

"Wait! Guess!" she said. "Come on, you'll never guess!"

"Is it a boy?" I said. I could tell from her voice that it was something silly like that. She sounded like Tara when she was always going on and on about Nikos last year.

"Yes!" she squealed. "But I mean, we're just friends. We're just going to the park. That's all."

"As long as it's not Brett Arbus," I said. "I nearly couldn't be friends with Kristal anymore when she had a crush on him last year. And I think he's dating Josephine now anyway."

"Ick, no," Rebekah said, which made me like her even more. "No, OK, I'll tell you. It's Eric!"

"Eric Lee?" I said. "That's awesome. He's cool."

Eric is one of Parker and Danny's best friends. He's really quiet, but I find quiet people kind of fascinating. Like, how do they stop themselves from talking? Aren't there things bouncing around in their heads all the time that they want to say? Everything I think seems to pop right out of my mouth, so when I meet people who don't do that, it totally confuses me.

"Well, we're just friends," Rebekah said again. "But he's bringing his dog and I'm bringing my dog, so . . ."

"I really gotta go," I said, hearing my mom call me again. "But have fun!"

"Good luck with your, uh . . . problem," Rebekah said. "Sorry I couldn't help."

"That's OK," I said, feeling sad again. "It probably wasn't a good idea anyway."

I hung up and ran downstairs with Yeti. Mom and Dad were sitting at the kitchen table with matching cups of coffee. They looked very serious.

"Hi, sweetheart," Dad said. "Want some cereal?"

"No thanks," I said. My stomach was tied in knots. I couldn't even think about food.

Yeti didn't have that problem, though. He trotted over to his bowl and stuck his nose into it, then looked up at me. I poured some dog food out for him and he started eating, *crunch crunch crunch.*

"Heidi," Mom said gently. "I think we've found the dog's owner."

"Already?" I cried. "But are you sure? Maybe it isn't them."

"Well, they're going to come over and see if they recognize him," Dad said. "That's the bad news."

"There's good news?" I said hopefully.

"They can't come until tomorrow," Mom said. "So you can spend the whole day today with Yeti, if you want."

I liked that Mom remembered his name. Except I guess it wasn't really his name. Tomorrow he'd have to go back to someone else's house and have a whole different name and different owners who couldn't possibly love him as much as I did. I only got one day to spend with my new best friend. That didn't sound like much good news to me.

I crouched down and gave Yeti a hug so Mom and Dad wouldn't see that I was close to crying.

"Hey, you know what?" Dad said. "I got some great travel books about India. We can talk about it tonight. There's this ghost town we can visit that was abandoned years and years ago — it sounds really cool."

I knew he was trying to cheer me up. I love looking forward to our trips. But right then I felt like I wouldn't be able to think about anything but Yeti ever again, and how sad and confused he would be about why I didn't want to keep him.

"Can I take Yeti to the park?" I said, my voice muffled by Yeti's fur.

"Sure, honey," said Mom. "Take my cell phone so you can call us if you need a ride home or anything."

I went back upstairs to change and call Danny. At least now I could finally meet his famously brilliant dog, Buttons. I didn't tell him that my parents had found Yeti's owners. I wanted to pretend, just for the day, that Yeti was really mine and we'd get to stay together forever.

When I got back downstairs, Mom had packed a lunch for me and a bag for Yeti with water and a tennis ball and a few biscuits. It nearly made me cry again. I had no idea my mom knew anything about taking care of a dog. Maybe she'd actually been listening while I watched all those dog shows on TV. Maybe she was more OK with the idea of me having a dog than she let me know.

But it didn't matter. I didn't want another dog. I wanted Yeti.

CHAPTER 12

Yeti had no idea that anything was wrong. He danced along the sidewalk next to me, grabbing the leash in his teeth and bumping into my legs with his head. I saw Avery watching from his window and I waved, but he barely waved back. I wished I could invite him to the park, but I knew his mom wouldn't let him go anywhere for at least a week after he got detention.

It was one of those ridiculously pretty October days where it's still sunny and blue and gold outside and you can't even imagine that winter is coming. Some of the leaves were turning orange and red, and the air smelled like bonfires and the last outdoor grilled hamburgers until May.

Yeti's fur was silky and shiny in the sunshine. He kept lifting his nose and inhaling like he wanted to gather up all the smells in the world. A stray red leaf whisked across the path in front of him, and he slapped it down with one big paw, then grinned at me like, *I'm pretty tough, aren't I?*

We got to the dog run in the park before anyone else — or at least, that's what I thought when I opened the gate. Then I realized that there was someone sitting on the bench at the far end. I might not even have noticed him, but his dog came galloping across the gravel to say hi to Yeti.

"Oh, hi!" I said, crouching to pet the new dog. It was one I'd never seen before. She was a small, perfectly gorgeous Sheltie with intelligent dark eyes and perked-up ears. She looked like a delicate miniature Lassie. Her white paws danced on the gravel as she darted around Yeti, trying to get close enough to sniff him without letting him sniff her. Yeti's ears flapped as he spun around, ready to play.

"Sorry," said the Sheltie's owner, hurrying up to us. It was a guy about my own age, but I'd never seen him before either. He had bright blue eyes and he was wearing a Buffalo Bills shirt with jeans, which was funny because we weren't anywhere near Buffalo. He needed a haircut; his brown hair was a little shaggy and he had a few strands tucked behind his ears to keep them out of his eyes.

"That's OK," I said. "What's your dog's name?"

"This is Jeopardy," he said, waving one hand at the Sheltie. "I'm Noah."

"Hi Noah," I said, sticking out my hand for him to shake. "I'm Heidi, and this is Yeti. Do you live around here?"

"Yeah," he said, rubbing the back of his neck and looking around. "I think so. I hope I can get home again."

I laughed, but then I stopped when I saw he looked serious. "Don't you know where you live?" I asked.

"We just moved here," he said, shoving his hands in his pockets. "I start school on Monday."

"Really?" I said. "But you missed the first month!"

Noah hunched his shoulders. "I know," he said. He didn't look as happy about that as I would be. One less month of school? That sounded fine by me!

"Well, you didn't miss anything important," I said. "Blah blah pyramids and South American geography and whatever. Hey, maybe you'll be in my class. Sixth grade? Westminster Elementary?"

Noah nodded. "Mr. Perry, I think," he said.

"Peary," I corrected him. "Oh, hey! That is my class! That's so cool! Mr. Peary is awesome!" I don't know why I got so excited; I think maybe I just wanted Noah to get excited, too, since he looked kind of nervous about starting a new school and I guess I would be, too. But I kind of jumped up and down and clapped my hands and then Yeti got excited, too, and he woofed and jumped on me and I fell over and ended up with both dogs on top of me somehow.

"Are you OK?" Noah said, pulling Jeopardy off me. He looked very concerned, but I couldn't stop laughing. I mean, what could be better than having a dog jump on you whenever you fall over? The way I see it, that maybe makes it look like you fell over on purpose to play with the dog.

"Yeah, I'm all right," I said, sitting up. I gave Yeti a big hug and he buried his face in my neck, panting happily.

"Your dog is enormous," Noah said, squatting beside us. Jeopardy sat next to him and put her paw on his knee like she thought he'd give her a treat if she did that, but he didn't.

"Isn't he huge?" I said, ruffling Yeti's fur. I didn't want to explain that he wasn't really my dog. I pointed to Noah's shirt. "Did you move here from Buffalo?"

"Rochester," Noah said, glancing down at the football jersey. "Close enough."

"You'll like it here," I said. "There are lots of kids with dogs. Some of my friends are coming now." I looked at my wrist, forgetting again that I'd lost my watch. "Um, sometime soon anyway. You can meet them and all their dogs, too."

Now Noah looked really nervous. "Um, actually, I gotta go home," he said, standing up. "I still have to unpack. My room is a mess."

"Oh, please," I said. "I am the queen of messy rooms. Are you sure you can't stay?"

"Sorry," he said, clipping a silver chain leash onto Jeopardy's collar. "But, uh, it was nice to meet you."

It was funny how polite he sounded. "Nice to meet you, too," I said. "Good luck finding your way home! See you in school on Monday!"

"Yup," he said, rubbing the back of his neck again. As he led her to the gate, Jeopardy looked back at us like she wanted to stay and play.

I noticed that Noah didn't talk to her at all. I'd yak-yak-yakked to Yeti the whole way here, like, "Ooo, what do you smell, is it amazing?" and "Good boy, peeing outside!" and "Hey, Yeti, maybe we should run away together, what do you think? But then I wouldn't get to go to India. And I really like my house and my parents and my friends. I just want to keep you, too! Come on, Yeti, help me brainstorm." Anyone who'd passed me on the street probably thought I was a lunatic.

Danny and Rosie and Buttons showed up about two minutes after Noah left. Buttons is an insanely adorable poodle puppy, all white fluff and sparkly black button eyes and turbocharged energy. Yeti fell madly in love with her on sight. She was only about the size of his head, but when she pounced on his paws, he rolled right over and let her climb on top of him.

Buttons flopped across his face and *rrrrrrr*ed triumphantly as if she'd managed to pin him down. He batted at her gently with his paws.

Then the gate squeaked and both of them bounced up with their tails wagging. Coming into the dog run were Eric and Rebekah. Eric turned bright red when he saw us, but Rebekah waved and smiled. Her little dog, Noodles, came bounding over and jumped on Buttons like they were old friends. In a second they were rolling around with their paws wrapped around each other. Yeti lowered his head and sniffed them curiously, like he was trying to figure out how one small furry friend had suddenly multiplied into two.

"Hey Eric," Danny said, raising his eyebrows at Rebekah.

"Hey *Danny*," Eric said, making the same face at

me. Danny cleared his throat and started talking about the weather really fast.

Eric's bulldog, Meatball, shambled over slowly, sniffing the ground every couple of steps. He rolled his eyes up at us in a *Hmmm, I don't know what I think of you* kind of way. But after I let him sniff my hand for about half an hour, he finally let me scratch him behind the ears. It seemed like he really liked that; he went *SNAAARRRRRZZZGARRRAAARRRR*, which sounded like growling, but Eric said that was his happy noise.

"Who are you?" Rosie said to Rebekah, a little bit rudely.

"You know Rebekah," I said. "She's in the same class as me and Danny."

"Huh," Rosie said, looking from her to Eric.

"I like your dog. She's really cute," Rebekah said to Rosie, and that seemed to get her on Rosie's good side.

We threw the ball for Buttons and Yeti. Yeti turned out to be great at fetching, just like Buttons — he brought the ball straight back to me, but he couldn't seem to figure out that he was supposed to drop it afterward. He poked my hand with his nose, but when I reached for the ball in his mouth, he jumped back. Or when I finally grabbed it, he'd hang on, so I had to wrestle it out of his jaws.

Danny laughed at us. "Your dog's a goof," he said to me.

"We'll have to work on that," I teased Yeti. And then I realized we wouldn't get to work on fetching. I wouldn't get to train him to drop the ball, or teach him to sit and roll over, or cuddle with him on the couch. After that night, I might not even see him again.

"Heidi?" Rebekah said as Danny ran off, chasing Buttons. "Are you OK? You look so sad all of a sudden."

"It's all right," I said. I didn't want to spend the day being sad. Or at least, I didn't want my friends to know how sad I was. "Come on, Yeti," I called. "Race you to the water fountain!"

I'd tell Rebekah and Danny about Yeti's real owners later.

For today, he was *my* dog.

CHAPTER 13

I didn't sleep much Saturday night. For one thing, I was too worried about meeting Yeti's real owners and finding out that they were as terrible as I was afraid they would be. For another, *somebody* kept hogging the whole bed.

When Yeti and I came downstairs in the morning, my dad was making blackberry pancakes, which are my favorite kind. His laptop was open on the table with a travel website about India on the screen. I clicked on a picture of something called the Qutb Minar, which looked like a big tower. I wondered how you were supposed to pronounce that.

Yeti was nearly tall enough to rest his head on the table while keeping all his paws on the floor. He came over and poked the table with his nose, blinking at the laptop. I reached for his collar and he jumped back, getting his paws tangled in the power cord. The laptop skidded across the table, and I just managed to catch it before it crashed to the floor.

Yeti looked surprised, like that couldn't possibly have been his fault. He picked up one front paw, then the other, sniffing them like they were big sausages he'd suddenly found at the end of his legs.

"It's OK, Yeti," I said, placing the laptop carefully back in the center of the table. "I know how you feel." If Yeti hadn't knocked over the laptop, I probably would have done it myself somehow.

Dad put the syrup on the table and looked down at me while I put my shoes on. "This is for the best, sweetheart," he said. "Can you imagine living in this house with a dog that big?"

I rumpled Yeti's fur. "He's a good dog, Dad. I could train him not to knock things over. I know I could."

He chuckled. "Honey, you can't even train *yourself* not to knock things over."

That was true. "Well, it's kind of hard when there are so many things just waiting to be knocked over," I pointed out. "But maybe he's smarter than I am."

We both looked at Yeti, who had moved on to sniffing his own tail with a befuddled expression on his face.

"Maybe not," my dad said with a smile. "Well, hurry up and take him out. The pancakes are almost ready." He unplugged the laptop and moved it to a shelf where it was safe from both me and Yeti.

I was about to clip on Yeti's leash when the doorbell rang.

Ding-dong! Ding-dong!

"WOOF! WOOF! WOOF! WOOF!" Yeti announced, leaping around in excitement. Dad whisked a plant out of the way before Yeti's exuberant tail could knock it over.

"Oh, no!" I cried. "It can't be them already!" Yeti came over and buried his nose in my hands, almost like he knew what I was feeling.

We left him at his food bowl and came out of the kitchen as my mom opened the front door. A scraggly-looking couple was standing on the doorstep. The guy had a thin wispy mustache the same color as his face. The woman's hair was flat and blond, and she was chewing gum. They were both wearing black rain boots and jeans with lots of holes in them.

"We're here for the dog," said the woman. She cracked her gum and peered over Mom's shoulder into the house.

My mom looked a little confused. "Sure, come on in," she said, stepping back.

"Nah, that's OK," said the guy. "We'll just take him and go. Rufus! Come on, Rufus!" He let out a weird airy whistle through his mustache.

Yeti came trotting out of the kitchen with his ears perked up. My heart sank. He knew that name, all right. But he stopped when he saw the couple, and then turned around and ran back into the kitchen.

"What'd you do to our dog?" the woman asked, squinting.

"Yeah, and where'd you find him anyway?" asked the guy. "I mean, it's kind of weird. He was tied up in the yard and everything. We've never had a dog escape before."

"My daughter found him in the park across from her school," my mom said. I could tell she was trying to be polite. "Do you have many dogs?"

"Yeah, we breed 'em," said the woman. "Newfies, Saint Bernards, pit bulls, all the big dogs. Whatever people want. Although this one we got from a friend, so we ain't had him long." She squinted at my mom again. "You looking for a dog? We got some good guard dogs."

Mom glanced at me. "Is, er . . . Rufus for sale?"

"No," the man said before I could get my hopes up. "He already has a buyer. We were supposed to get rid of him two weeks ago. Rufus! Come *here*! More trouble than he's worth," he muttered. "I should charge double."

"He didn't have a collar when I found him," I said. "You should give all your dogs collars. And microchips. In case they get lost."

The woman gave me a mean look. "Or stolen," she said.

"Like I said, they don't usually get loose," the guy added. "We've got about twenty of them tied up in the yard or in the crates back there most of the time, and this is the first time I've seen one get out."

Poor Yeti. Tied up with twenty other dogs and nobody to love him. He must have been very clever to escape them. Part of me wished I were as brave and dumb as Avery right now, so I could kick them both and not care what happened afterward. But I'd never actually do something like that.

"Heidi, go get the dog," Mom said.

"I should give the leash back to Parker," I said.

The man handed me a collar and leash already hooked together. I turned them over in my hands and realized it was a choke collar, with bits that would stick into the dog's neck if he tried to pull. I gave Dad a horrified look and saw that he was looking at the collar, too.

"Go on, Heidi," my mom said.

I walked slowly back into the kitchen. Yeti was under the table, pressed into the corner. He lowered his head and peeked out at me under the white-and-pink tablecloth. I got down on my knees and crawled in next to him.

Arroorrrrooof. Yeti lay down and put his head on my knee. His big brown eyes looked up at me trustingly. How could I put this collar on him and give him back to those people?

I wondered what would happen if I just opened the back door and let him run off again. Would he know to run and hide? Would he come back? What if they caught him as he ran down the driveway?

I buried my hands in his fur and rubbed his back. I knew they were all waiting for me. But I couldn't do it. I wished I could stay under the table with Yeti forever.

I saw my dad's black sneakers come in from the den and walk over to us. He crouched beside the table and rested his elbows on his knees, looking at me and Yeti.

"Dad," I said, but I couldn't talk, or else I'd start to cry.

"Honey, listen," he said. "Do you really want this dog? This particular dog?"

I nodded really hard. Yeti's tail thumped on the floor.

Dad glanced down at his hands. "What if it meant we couldn't go to India next year?"

I rubbed my eyes. "Why?"

His voice got quieter. "We asked how much it would cost to buy him, and they said we'd have to pay more than the other buyer. It would take a bite out of our travel savings. We'd have to spend the summer at home instead. But if you really want him . . ."

"Yes!" I blurted. My head was spinning. I couldn't believe my parents had even asked — that there was even a chance they'd say yes, let alone give up their trip for my dog. "I'd rather have Yeti, more than anything in the world. Oh, please, Dad, please please please —"

"All right, give me that," he said, holding out his hand. I passed him the choke collar and chain. He winked at me as he got up and went back into the den.

I felt like I couldn't breathe. I wrapped my arms around Yeti and held on tight, wishing and hoping that I wouldn't suddenly wake up and find out this was all a dream.

It seemed like a few centuries went by. Maybe a few thousand years. Maybe the entire age of the universe. The Egyptians could have built four hundred pyramids in the time we spent under the table, waiting in agony.

But finally I heard the front door close. Mom and Dad came back into the kitchen. They both crouched beside the table.

"Thank you, Mom," I whispered.

Aaaoooorrrrrooof, Yeti agreed.

"I'm still not sure this is a good idea," Mom said, but she was smiling. She reached under the table and stroked Yeti's long, soft fur. "But I think we're stuck with him now."

CHAPTER 14

I probably shouldn't tell you about the glass giraffe we broke or the bowl of pancake batter we knocked over while Yeti and I were leaping around the kitchen celebrating.

"Oh, dear," my mom said, pressing her hands to her head while I ran around trying to clean up the mess. "Arthur, what are we going to do with these two?"

"Maybe it's time to make the house a bit safer for the clumsier members of the family," Dad said.

"Really?" I said. "Could we? I swear, I'm sure I wouldn't break things so much if there weren't so many things to break!" That sentence made a lot more sense in my head.

"Well," Mom said thoughtfully, "I do like the living room the way it is. But perhaps we could make the den a bit more Heidi-friendly."

"And Yeti-friendly," added Dad. "We don't have to keep the Orrefors vases or Chihuly glass flowers in there. They could go in the sala."

Mom glanced around the kitchen. "Who really needs crystal bowls anyway?" she said. "We can store them in the dining room sideboard for special occasions."

"And there are a couple of pieces in the den that would look lovely in the museum," Dad suggested. "Or at my office."

"You'll be lucky," Mom said with a laugh.

"WOOF!" Yeti barked happily, and then his long swooping tail swept our basket of keys and gloves and mail onto the floor with a *crash*.

"All right, get out of here," Mom said, making shooing motions with her hands. "Give us a chance to save the artwork before we're arrested for destroying national treasures."

As she fluttered into the den, my dad patted my shoulder and whispered, "I never liked that green vase anyway."

Yeti and I nearly flew across the grass to Avery's back door. Kelly answered after a couple of knocks. She gave Yeti a startled look.

"What is *that*?" she asked.

"This is my new dog," I said proudly. "His name is Yeti. Isn't he wonderful? Can I take him upstairs to see Avery?"

Kelly pressed her lips together. "I suppose so," she

said. "But he'd better be doing homework when you get up there."

I hurried up the dark stairs to Avery's room. I didn't go into their house very often, unless Kelly was having a party of some sort. Usually we hang out in the yard or at my house.

"Guess what?" I yelped, throwing his door open.

Avery jumped a mile. He was totally not doing homework. He was watching an old episode of *Heroes* on the TV at the end of his bed.

Yeti galloped into the room and sailed onto the bed, scrambling over Avery's feet.

"Hey, watch it," Avery grumbled. But he reached out and scratched Yeti's ears, and Yeti flopped over onto his lap, offering his belly to be rubbed.

I closed the door quickly behind me in case Kelly was coming up the stairs. "You'll get in trouble if she sees you doing that," I said, nodding at the TV.

"What, more trouble?" Avery said sarcastically, hitting the mute button. "Oh, *no*. That would be *terrible*."

"So guess what?" I said, climbing onto the bottom of the bed. But I couldn't wait for him to guess — or, knowing Avery, make sarcastic comments instead. "Mom and Dad are letting me keep Yeti!" I burst out. "He's mine! For real! We bought him from his owners and everything!"

Yeti rolled back onto his paws and jumped off the bed. He started sniffing around the room. It wasn't as messy as my room, but it wasn't neat either. And it was really dark, because Avery kept all the shades down all the time. The only light came from his desk lamp and the glow of the TV.

"Wow," Avery said in a flat voice. "That's unexpected."

There's a photo frame that sits on the table beside Avery's bed. Normally he keeps it tipped over so you can't see the picture, but today it was upright. I picked it up and tilted it toward the light.

I knew what it was, of course, but I hadn't seen it in a while. It's a photo of me and Avery when we were both eight years old. We're crouching in the grass in my backyard, pointing at the camera because we're trying to get Avery's dog, Stitch, to look at the camera, too. But he's too busy licking Avery's face to pay attention, and we're all laughing, so it's a pretty silly picture of all of us.

Stitch was a mutt — a crazy, hyperactive, funny brown-and-white dog with pointy ears and scruffy terrier fur. Kelly bought him for Avery when she remarried his dad and they were all supposed to be a happy family again. Avery named him after the alien in *Lilo and Stitch*, which was one of our favorite movies of all time.

Stitch wasn't exactly a *good* dog. He was kind of like Avery that way. He got into mischief and barked at nothing and tried to pick fights with dogs way bigger than him. But he loved Avery like crazy. He followed Avery everywhere. And I got to play with them all the time.

But then Kelly and Avery's dad started fighting again, and for some reason that made Stitch act even more hyper and crazy and bad. Soon after they got divorced for a second time, Kelly decided she couldn't handle "that monstrous little dog" anymore. While Avery was at school one day, she took Stitch to a shelter, and we never saw him again.

Isn't that the saddest story ever? I cried for days when Mom told me. I cried so much, she actually got the name of the shelter from Kelly and drove me out there to say good-bye to Stitch. But he'd already been adopted by someone else by the time we got there. That's the only good part of the story. At least he found a new home, and the shelter people said it was somewhere he'd be happy.

That didn't make Avery feel any better, though. I knew he missed Stitch something awful. That's why, whenever he's a huge jerk at school, I try not to get mad. I try to think about how I would feel if someone took away the dog I loved so much. That's why what

I said to him that first week of school was so mean and I felt so bad about it.

I put the photo back down on the bedside table. Yeti had his head and shoulders all the way under the bed and was scrabbling around like he'd found buried treasure.

"I know it won't be like having Stitch back," I said. "But I hope you'll help me take care of Yeti. We can take him to the park together, like we used to. And you can come over anytime you want to hang out with him. He thinks you're pretty cool."

"I *am* pretty cool," Avery said.

I laughed. "Well, sure."

He gave me a sideways look. "I bet you just got this dog as an excuse to hang out with me more. I'm onto you, Tyler."

"Yeah, you got me," I said, grinning.

"Stay here for a second," he said, swinging his legs off the bed. "I gotta get something."

He left the room and I leaned over to check on Yeti. He was scratching at something that was pinned between the bed and the wall. I climbed over and dug my hand down into the gap. I felt something soft and furry under my fingers.

I pulled it out and gasped. I recognized it right

away. A small black-and-white stuffed dog with floppy ears.

"Arfer!"

Yeti jumped onto the bed and tried to take Arfer in his mouth. I held the stuffed animal out of his reach and looked at it more closely. It was definitely the dog I'd given Avery, like, seven years ago. I couldn't believe he still had it. It couldn't have been stuck back there this whole time. His mom changed the sheets every week; she would definitely have found it. So . . . did that mean Avery had kept it on purpose . . . and still slept with it?

I heard his footsteps coming back. He would *not* be happy if I teased him about this. Quickly I stuffed Arfer back behind the bed. Yeti whined and pawed at the wall, but I distracted him by throwing a blanket over his head. When Avery came in, Yeti was rolling and snuffling under the covers.

"Oh, thanks," Avery said. "I made that bed this morning, you know."

"Really?" I said. "I couldn't tell."

"Here." He tossed me an old, squeaky dog toy shaped like a floppy green frog. It had been Stitch's favorite toy.

Yeti surged out of the blankets and pounced on it

immediately. He seized it between his teeth and shook it like a piñata that he was hoping would explode into candy pieces.

"He loves it!" I said. "Are you sure he can have it? You don't mind?"

Avery shrugged. "Yeah, it's fine. Whatever."

"He might destroy it," I warned. "He's more destructive than he realizes."

"Well, you know all about that," Avery said.

I rubbed Yeti's soft head. "Right, so I know he *wants* to be a good dog. Right, Yeti?" Yeti dropped the frog for a minute to slurp his big pink tongue up the side of my face. "But I'll take him to classes and we'll practice tricks and he'll learn all the things I've seen dogs do on TV and then he'll be just perfect, I know it."

Avery actually laughed. "I'll believe that when I see it," he said.

"OK," I said. "Maybe not *perfect*. But that's all right. He doesn't have to be perfect all the time." Yeti's tail wagged, and he gave me a look like, *Well, that's lucky, because I don't see that happening!* "Clearly that's not a requirement for my friends," I teased Avery.

"Ha-ha," Avery said.

Yeti poked his shaggy head under my arm and I gave him a hug. "Don't worry, Yeti. We can be not-perfect together. That's what being best friends is all about."

Jeopardy is a great dog . . . when she isn't getting into trouble!

Pet Trouble

Smarty-Pants Sheltie

Turn the page for a sneak peek!

At last it was my turn. I was pretty nervous because Jeopardy was quietly freaking out. She couldn't take her eyes off the hurdle. I heard her go "ooorf! rroorrf!" in this tiny whimper kind of way while she watched the other dogs. Her white front paws went up and down, up and down on the rubber floor beside me, like she was practicing dance steps in her head or getting ready to start a race. By the time Alicia called us, Jeopardy was up on her back paws and straining at the end of her leash. As I stepped forward, she went: "ARF! ARF!" like she was shouting: "FINALLY! FINALLY!"

I stopped in front of the hurdle. Jeopardy's whole furry body was quivering with excitement. I leaned down to unclip her leash.

"OK, Jeopardy — " I started, but before I could say "over!" — actually, before I even finished her name — Jeopardy was gone. She leaped over that first hurdle and kept going. *Zip!* She went over the second hurdle. *Swish!* She flew over the third hurdle. "ARF ARF ARF ARF ARF!" she barked as she jumped, and then she kept barking at the top of her lungs as she bolted around the room.

"ARF ARF ARF ARF ARF ARF ARF ARF ARF!" She galloped in a huge circle around all of us, barking frantically.

"Jeopardy!" I yelled. "Get over here!"

"ARF ARF ARF ARF ARF!" she answered, flying like the wind from one wall to another. She looked both blissful and smugly triumphant, like she'd managed to fool me and escape and now she was having the time of her life.

I wanted to sink into the floor. Rosie put her hands on her hips like she'd never seen anything so disorderly in her life. She looked even more disapproving than Alicia.

"Jeopardy, come!" Alicia said firmly.

"ARF ARF ARF!" Jeopardy barked, darting forward and then dashing out of reach again as Alicia reached for her. Eric and Rebekah had their hands over their ears. Heidi and Ella were laughing hysterically.

"Jeopardy!" I shouted. "Stop! Stay!" I ran at her, but she ducked away from me, too. I threw myself forward to grab her collar and missed. My chin hit the bouncy floor with a painful *thwack*.

"Oh my gosh!" Heidi cried, clapping her hands to her mouth. "Noah, are you OK?"

"Yeah," I said, although my jaw hurt like crazy. Jeopardy stopped and stared at me from a few feet away.

"Aw, see, she feels bad," Heidi said, clasping her hands together.

I wasn't so sure about that. Her face was more like, *Why did you stop playing? What's wrong with you? Why are you so lame?*

"Come here!" I said.

"ARF!" Jeopardy answered and ran off with her tail wagging.

"Here," Parker said, handing Merlin's leash to Danny. "Let's corner her." He chased Jeopardy around the shiny blue tunnel. She raced toward the wall and we both ran at her from either side. Even so, she nearly slipped through our hands again, but I threw my arms over her back and tackled her to the floor.

Immediately she relaxed. As I lay on top of her, gasping for air, she craned her head back and licked my ear. "Ruff," she said calmly, like: *So that was fun. Now what?*

"Thanks," I said to Parker. He took the leash out of my hand and snapped it onto Jeopardy's collar.

"No problem," he said. He shook his brown hair out of his eyes and patted Jeopardy's head. "That's totally happened to me with Merlin."

I glanced over at the perfect golden retriever as I got to my feet. Merlin was sitting next to Danny with his head tilted curiously, as if he was wondering whether it would be safe to join our game or if Jeopardy was too insane.

“Really?” I said. It was hard to imagine having to chase Merlin down.

Parker rolled his eyes. “You have no idea,” he said.

I dragged Jeopardy back to our spot. Alicia was waiting with her eyebrows raised.

“I’m sorry,” I said.

“Don’t be,” she said. “I think it’s a good sign that she’s excited about the equipment. She’s a very smart little dog. But we might have to leave her leash on for a while, at least at first, so we don’t have to chase her every time.”

“Aww,” Danny said. “But it’s so funny to watch!” He imitated Jeopardy’s face as she ran away from us.

Everyone laughed. Ella leaned over to whisper something to Heidi. I was sure they were talking about what a terrible dog owner I was. It didn’t help me at all that Jeopardy was a “very smart little dog”; as far as I could tell, that just made me look even dumber next to her. I’d much prefer an ordinary-smart dog like Merlin or Yeti.

My face felt like it was burning up. Nobody else had to leave their dog’s leash on. Nobody else had a crazy dog like mine. Nobody else’s dog took up all the class time by acting like a lunatic.

Why was *my* dog always the worst behaved?